# Launching All Dogs

At that very moment, my thoughts were interrupted by the sound of a vehicle. An unauthorized vehicle was approaching our ranch headquarters compound. Even though I was in the middle of the Murphy Case, I had to tear myself away and find out who had entered our territory without permission.

"Come on, Drover, we've got a trespasser on the ranch! It's time to launch all dogs!"

He was still scratching his ear. "Yeah, but what about this itch?"

"Bring it along. We might have to use it for evidence later on."

And with that, we launched ourselves into the morning breeze and went streaking up the hill to find out just what the heck was going on. Little did we suspect . . . well, you'll see.

# The Case of
# the Shipwrecked Tree

# The Case of
# the Shipwrecked Tree

## John R. Erickson

Illustrations by Gerald L. Holmes

Puffin Books

# The Case of
# the Shipwrecked Tree

PUFFIN BOOKS
Published by the Penguin Group
Penguin Putnam Books for Young Readers,
345 Hudson Street, New York, New York 10014, U.S.A.
Penguin Books Ltd,
80 Strand, London WC2R ORL, England
Penguin Books Australia Ltd, 250 Camberwell Road,
Camberwell, Victoria 3124, Australia
Penguin Books Canada Ltd,
10 Alcorn Avenue, Toronto, Ontario, Canada M4V 3B2
Penguin Books (N.Z.) Ltd,
182-190 Wairau Road, Auckland 10, New Zealand

Penguin Books Ltd, Registered Offices:
Harmondsworth, Middlesex, England

Published simultaneously by Viking and Puffin Books,
divisions of Penguin Putnam Books for Young Readers, 2003

5  7  9  10  8  6  4

LIBRARY OF CONGRESS CATALOGING-IN-PUBLICATION DATA
Erickson, John R., date
The case of the shipwrecked tree / by John R. Erickson ;
illustrations by Gerald L. Holmes
p.  cm. — (Hank the cowdog ; 41)
Summary: Hank and Little Alfred get into trouble while playing pirates.
ISBN 0-670-03603-X — ISBN 0-14-230225-2 (pbk.)
[1. Dogs—Fiction.  2. Ranch life—West (U.S.)—Fiction.  3. West (U.S.)—Fiction.
4. Humorous stories.] I. Holmes, Gerald L., ill.  II. Title.
PZ7.E72556 Cark 2003  [Fic]—dc21  2002017930

Hank the Cowdog® is a registered trademark of John R. Erickson.

Printed in the United States of America

*For Rooster and Jody.*

# CONTENTS

# CHAPTER ONE

# We Learn about the Turkey Rebellion

It's me again, Hank the Cowdog. The Case of the Shipwrecked Tree began in the spring of the year, as I recall. Yes, of course it did. Drover and I never would have joined up with a pirate captain in the wintertime, because, well, who wants to make an ocean voyage when it's cold? Not me.

But that came after we got the news about the Turkey Rebellion. Have we discussed that? Maybe not. It was a pretty scary deal . . . but maybe we'd better slow down and take things one at a time.

Okay, it was spring. Warm days, chilly nights, spring foliage on all the trees. The buzzards, kites, sparrows, and cardinals had returned to the ranch after spending the winter . . . somewhere. Down south, I suppose.

1

Why do they leave every fall? I have no idea. Ask a bird. I consider it a huge waste of time and effort. Come spring, they just turn around and fly right back. Dumb birds.

What's the point? If they don't like it around here, why do they keep coming back, and if they do like it here, why do they always leave? It makes no sense to me, but let me hasten to point out that I'm not a bird. Maybe you had already noticed that.

Where were we? Oh yes. Birds. Every year in the fall, our summer birds leave and fly south. We don't know why and we don't care, but some birds stay here over the winter. One type of bird that stays on the ranch year-round is the wild turkey.

Most of the time, your wild turkeys are okay birds. They don't bother me and I don't bother them. They run in flocks, roost in cottonwood trees, and steal grain from the horses, which is fine with me because I'm not fond of horses. However—

There's always a "however," isn't there? I had never supposed that our local turkey population might be involved in a sophisticated spying operation until . . .

It all began in the early morning hours, as I recall. I was sitting at my desk in the Security Division's Vast Office Complex beneath the gas tanks, going over some files and reports. I had hardly slept in days, I mean, the routine of running the ranch had kept me up day and night for so long, I couldn't even remember the last time I'd grabbed a nap.

You might say I was "off duty," but that doesn't mean much. In this line of work, there is no "off duty." If we're not working traffic on the county road or guarding the chicken house or checking out enemy spies, we're back at the office, reading reports.

That's what I was doing—slumped over my desk and reading a Monster Report, #MR-1055327—when all at once, Drover came bursting in.

"Hank, come quick! The wild turkeys are coming right up to the gas tanks! I tried to bark 'em away, but one of 'em pecked me on the nose."

"Hose nose snorking mork beetlebomb."

"I thought you'd want to know, and maybe you'd better wake up."

"I can't wake up, Drivel, because I'm not asniggle."

"Yeah, you are asleep. I can tell, 'cause you're stretched out on your gunnysack and your eyes are closed. You can't fool me."

I turned toward the sound of his voice and tried to beam him a gaze of purest steel, but the office was totally dark and I couldn't see him. "Churn on the lice, Droving, I'm having trouble bubble guttersniping the hogwash."

"I'm right here, if you'll just open your eyes."

Suddenly, I realized that something was wrong, badly wrong. I leaped to my feet, staggered three steps to the north, and collapsed again. "Holy strokes, Dobber, I've been blinded! I fought them off as long as I could, but the turkeys kept coming for our pork chops!"

"My name's Drover."

Suddenly my eyes . . . hmmm, my eyes popped open, almost as though they'd been closed, and all at once I saw light and objects and . . . hmmm, a smallish white dog with a stub tail. "Who are you and why are you honking the catfish bait?"

"Well . . . I'm not sure about that, but I'm Drover. Remember me? I'm your best friend."

I blinked my eyes and struggled to my feet. "Yes, of course. How badly am I hurt?"

He gave me a foolish grin. "Well . . . I don't think you're hurt at all. I think maybe you were asleep and you're not awake yet."

I staggered two steps to the west. The bleeding had stopped and my legs seemed to be working. "For your information, I was *not* asleep. I was reading a monster report and . . ." I shot a glance over my shoulder. "Wait a second. You're Drover, aren't you? Welcome back, son. How was Cowabonga? You went on a trip, right?"

"Not me. I've been here forever."

"Just as I thought." I blinked my eyes and shook the vapors out of my head. My mind began to climb back into the driver's seat of my . . . something. "Okay, Drover, I'm beginning to see a pattern here. I was reading files and reports, and something caused me to lose consciousness."

"Yeah, you fell asleep."

"It wasn't that simple, Drover. There's always more. These things are never as simple as we think."

"I'll be derned."

I began pacing, as I often do when my mind is beginning to focus like a laser bean. "My guess is that they broke into the office and sprinkled *sleeping powder* on those files. How else can you explain my sudden loss of consciousness?"

"Who's 'they'?"

"*They*, Drover, our enemies. They're clever beyond your wildest dreams, and they have agents and spies at work around the clock. Have you seen any strangers in the last two hours?"

"Well, let me think. Oh yeah, I saw some turkeys, and that's what I came to tell you. There are some turkeys lurking around the gas tanks."

I stopped pacing and pondered his words.

"*Turkeys lurking?* Drover, this is just a hunch, but I have a feeling that there's some hidden meaning behind those words. Did you notice that they rhyme?"

His eyes lit up. "Yeah, and you know what else? If one of the turkeys was named Murphy, it would rhyme even better: Murphy Turkey Lurking."

"Drover, please try to be . . ." I ran those words back and forth through my mind. "Murphy Turkey Lurking. Hmmm. You know, you might have stumbled onto something important. Those three words have a very suspicious ring, almost as though they were meant to go together."

"Yeah, and I came up with 'em all by myself."

"Don't get carried away, son. This is just the tip of the ice pick. The question we must ask ourselves now is 'Why are the turkeys lurking?' Is it possible that they're plotting a rebellion?"

"Well, let's see here . . ."

"And who is this Murphy character?"

"Well . . ." Drover rolled his eyes around. "You don't reckon he might be . . . a spy, do you?"

I glared at the runt. "A spy? Don't be absurd. Turkeys are harmless birds, and also they're not very smart. Nobody would recruit a turkey to be a spy. In other words, no. Your theory doesn't cut water."

"Oh drat." His face fell into a heap of wrinkles, but then he brightened. "Wait a second. What if he's not a turkey at all, but he's a spy . . . wearing a turkey suit?"

I couldn't help laughing. "Drover, sometimes you say the craziest—a spy wearing a turkey suit? Ha, ha! Why, that's . . ." I gave it some thought. "On the other hand, it would be clever, wouldn't it? I mean, nobody would ever suspect . . . it's just the sort of trick "they" might come up with. Of course! A Turkey Rebellion! You know, Drover, you might have just blown this case wide open."

All at once he was hopping up and down. "Oh goodie, I'm so happy!"

"But once again, we can't allow ourselves to get carried away. For you see, Drover, our work on this case has just begun." I shot a glance at the wild turkeys. All at once they looked very suspicious. "We need a volunteer."

His smile faded. "Oops. You mean . . ."

"Yes, Drover, you've been chosen, out of all the dogs in the world, to volunteer for a very important mission."

"Well, you know, I'd love to volunteer, but this old leg sure has—"

"It's a great opportunity, son. It'll give you a chance to prove who you really are."

8

"Yeah, but I already know. I'm the one who's scared of turkeys."

"Rubbish. Turkeys are harmless. Now listen carefully." I glanced over my shoulders and dropped my voice to a hoist . . . to a whisper, let us say. "Go back out there and infilterate their group. Be polite, turn on your charm, get to know them and win their confidence. Listen to their conversation and try to determine which one is Murphy the Spy. When you get a positive ID, come back and we'll plan our next move."

"Well . . . if you really think I can do it. Should I pretend that I'm a turkey?"

"No, I don't think that would work. Your legs are too short, and you've got a stub tail. Just pretend you're a dog—a dog who wants to get to know a few turkeys."

"I think I can do it, 'cause I really am a dog."

"Right. Good luck, soldier. I'll stay here at Command Central and man the rodeo."

"You mean the radio?"

"That's what I said. I'll stay here and man the radio."

"Yeah, but you're not a man."

"All right, Drover, I'll stay here and *dog* the radio. Now get moving. We'll meet back here at oh-eight hundred."

"Okay, here I go!"

I watched as he went skipping away—a happy little dog who had found a place for himself in the big wide world. I felt a glow of fatherly pride, knowing that I had helped bring a small ray of meaning into the garbage heap of his life.

Then he disappeared from sight and I was alone again—alone with my thoughts and the mementos of a long and glorious career, alone in the echoing chambers of the Security Division's Vast Office Complex. I heaved a sigh and returned to the grinding routine of . . . snork murk snickelfritz . . . ZZZZZZZZZZZZZZZZZZZZZZZZZZZZZZZZZZZ ZZZZZZZZZZZZZZZZ.

CHAPTER TWO

# Murphy the Spy

I fought sleep as long as I could, but there are two powerful forces in this world that a dog can't resist. The first is sleep, and I don't remember the second one.

So, yes, my struggle against the forces of sleep was doomed to fail, and after minutes and minutes of fighting to stay awake, I must have slipped the surly bonds of Life and sailed out into the misty harbor of delicious sleep.

It was wonderful! All the weeks and weeks of sleepless nights, all the cares and worries of running the Security Division, all the frayed nerves and knotted muscles melted away like . . . something. Mothballs in a pouring rain, I suppose, or maybe snowballs in a pouring rain.

11

Sugar cubes in a cup of hot tea.

Graham crackers in a glass of milk.

They all melted away, is the point, and there for a few moments, I felt myself . . . Suddenly a voice cut through the silence.

"Hi Hank, I'm back."

I jacked myself up to a sitting position and began the backbreaking process of cranking open my eyelids. There stood Drover—grinning, happy, and dumb. And wigwagging his stub tail. "Werewolfs wear rumple buckets—you just left. How could you be back so snooze?"

"Well, I made friends with the turkeys and got 'em to tell me everything."

"Talkies? What are you turking about?"

"Turkeys, wild turkeys. See, you sent me on an important mission to incinerate the turkeys, and I did and now I'm back."

"Yes, of course. Be still a minute and let me think. And stop wagging your tail. It hurts my ears." I walked several steps away and filled my lungs with carbon diego. My private moments were over. I had been pulled back into the world of worry, care, and responsibility. I walked back toward the little runt. "All right, Drover, I'm ready to hear your report."

"Gosh, did you fall asleep again?"

"No, I did not. I was merely . . . give me your report on the turkey spies. Did you find Murphy?"

He sat down and started scratching his ear. "Oh yeah, I spotted him right away. He was the one who looked just like a turkey."

"So we were right, weren't we? He came onto the ranch in that turkey costume and thought we'd never notice. Ha! What a foolish spy. Why are you scratching your ear?"

"Oh, because it itches . . . I guess. And it feels better when I scratch it."

"I would be grateful if you'd scratch on your own time. Scratching in public is rude and uncouth."

"Oh, sorry."

"Go on with your report. Did you hear any of their plans? What is Murphy up to? Surely he came here on some kind of devilish mission."

"Oh yeah, I heard 'em talking, and I think Murphy came here on some kind of . . ." He paused for a moment. ". . . devilish mission."

Those words sent a shock all the way out to the end of my tail, but I tried to conceal it. "I'm not surprised, Drover. That's exactly what I had feared and expected. Okay." I began pacing back and forth in front of him. "Let's get down to pacifics. Tell me everything you know."

"Well, let's see. It's a big ocean and it's over by California."

"Ocean, California. Got it. Go on."

"It's full of salt and seaweed and . . . and jellyfish."

"Jellyfish, huh? This is getting interesting. Jellyfish have poison stingers, you know. Is it possible that Murphy has developed some kind of new high-tech weapon that fires jellyfish instead of bullets? They're very slippery, you know."

"Yeah, they're made of jelly."

"The spies, Drover. Spies are very slippery characters."

"Boy, I love jelly."

"Exactly. Well, this is pretty scary, Drover. You actually heard the turkeys discussing this new jellyfish technology?"

"Well . . . I'm not sure about that."

I stopped pacing and studied the runt. "Did you or not? If you didn't, why are we discussing jellyfish?"

He rolled his eyes around. "Well, I was kind of wondering that myself. You wanted me to talk about the ocean and . . . well, I couldn't think of anything to say, but I figured jellyfish live in the ocean. I guess."

"Drover, is this some kind of pathetic attempt at humor? If it is, I must warn you that the punishment for making jokes during a briefing is very severe."

"Maybe I heard you wrong."

I began pacing again. "In that case, we'll disregard all references to the bogus jellyfish technology and plunge on with your report. What I'm looking for, Drover, is *specific* information. Details."

"I got de-tailed when I was a pup, and I've had a stub ever since."

"I'm not interested in your stub tail."

"Neither am I, but I have to wear it every day."

"Drover, does your stub tail relate to this particular Turkey Report? If not, then let's move along."

"Well, when I'm out with a bunch of turkeys, I always notice that they've got beautiful tails made of feathers, and mine's just a stub. It makes me feel like I've got . . ." A quiver came into his voice. ". . . an inferior tail."

I stopped pacing and turned slowly to face him. "Drover, you *do* have an inferior tail. It's not a feeling or an illusion. It's a fact. You'll never have a beautiful feathered turkey tail, and the sooner you accept yourself as you really are, the quicker you'll be. Now, can we get on with this briefing?"

He hung his head and sniffled. "I guess so, but sometimes it gets me down."

"I'm sorry."

"Are you really?"

"No. Hurry up." I began pacing again. "Tell me exactly what Murphy said. I want his exact precise words, and omit all references to jellyfish and your tail."

"Well, okay, let me think here." He squeezed one eye shut and wadded up the left side of his mouth. It appeared that he was probing the empty depths of his mind, which was encouraging. "Here we go. His exact words were: 'Gobble gobble gobble-gobble gobble gobble-gobble-gobble.'"

"That's what he said? Are you sure about that?"

"Yep, I heard it with my own ears. What does it mean?"

"It means . . ." I cut my eyes from side to side. "It means, Drover, that we will now sing 'The Turkey Song.'"

"'The Turkey Song'? I never heard of it."

"Then listen and take notes."

And with that, before Drover's very ears, I sang this song.

## The Turkey Song

There are turkeys lurking in the murky
    shadows of the ranch.
We have reason to suppose that they are
    waiting for a chance
To invade the place and take control.
    Their leader's in disguise.
He's the famous secret agent, name of
    Murphy Turkey Spy!

He's a dangerous fellow, an ace of illusion,
Who seems to delight in creating confusion.

**17**

But Drover and I are working the case.
This Turkey Rebellion won't get to first base.

But it's really confusing and we can't decide
If this Murphy's a human in turkey disguise,
Or an agent who's pulling the ultimate sham:
A turkey disguised just to be who he am.

There are turkeys lurking in the murky
    shadows just outside.
We can hear their "gobble, gobble," as they
    try to scheme and hide.
They might think that they have tricked us
    with their foolish follyrot
But we've solved this case: we know they're
    either turkeys . . . or they're not.

When I had finished the song (pretty awesome song, huh?) . . . when I had so-forthed the so forth, I noticed that Drover was looking at me with a goofy expression.

"Why are you staring at me like that?"

"Well . . . I guess I'm confused. You think maybe Murphy's not really a spy and . . . maybe I didn't really see him?"

I heaved a sigh. "No, no, no. That's what they *want* us to think, Drover. As I've told you many times before, never fall for the obvious. In this business, the more absurd things appear to be, the closer they are to Reality as It Really Is."

"Well, this is pretty absurd."

"Exactly my point. Reason and common sense tell us that there is no Murphy, no ring of turkey spies, no dark conspiracy to overthrow the ranch, but that should be a warning."

"You mean—"

"Yes, Drover. Murphy is here on the ranch. Now that he knows we're after him, it'll be twice as hard to lure him into a trap. This is going to be a very difficult case."

Drover's eyes grew wide with fear. "Gosh, what'll we do?"

I plundered that for a moment. *Pondered*, I should say. "We'll carry on as though nothing has happened, as though we don't suspect a thing. If we're lucky, he'll get careless and expose himself through a mistake."

Drover gave his head a shake. "Well . . . he sure looked like a turkey."

"He's clever, no question about it, but don't forget this: the turkier they look, the spyer they are. You can put that into your pipe and blow bubbles with it." I noticed that his eyes had crossed. "Please don't cross your eyes in the middle of my lecture."

"I think I'm confused. Can I go back to bed?"

"I'm afraid not, son. Until we break this case and expose Murphy the Spy, neither of us will be getting much sleep."

"Well, can I scratch my ear?"

I gave that some thought. "Okay, go ahead, if it'll make you feel better. Oh, and Drover, don't feel too bad about being confused. This guy's a real pro. Even I might have been thrown off the track of the train."

At that very moment, my thoughts were interrupted by the sound of a vehicle. An unauthorized vehicle was approaching our ranch headquarters compound. Even though I was in the middle of the Murphy Case, I had to tear myself away and find out who had entered our territory without permission.

"Come on, Drover, we've got a trespasser on the ranch! It's time to launch all dogs!"

He was still scratching his ear. "Yeah, but what about this itch?"

"Bring it along. We might have to use it for evidence later on."

And with that, we launched ourselves into the morning breeze and went streaking up the hill to find out just what the heck was going on. Little did we suspect . . . well, you'll see.

# CHAPTER THREE

# We Capture the Mailman

D o I dare let you in on the procedures we followed on this assignment? I've already mentioned that we "launched all dogs," but there was quite a bit more to it than that. And some of it was pretty technical and complicated.

What do you think? Let's give it a try.

Okay, the first report of the tresspassing vehicle came in at 0831. At 0832 I put the ranch under Red Alert and gave the order to launch all dogs. At precisely 0833 Drover and I left the Security Division's Vast Office Complex, taxied into the wind, and went to Full Throttle on all engines. It was a successful launch—smoke, flames, a deafening roar, the whole nine yards—and by 0834 we were streaking northward on a course of oh-five-zirro-zirro.

(Just a brief note here. Ordinary dogs who do ordinary things would express that compass heading as "oh-five-zero-zero." But those of us who've spent years in this line of work have found that saying "zirro-zirro" instead of "zero-zero" just—well, it sounds better, more official. Don't you agree? Of course you do).

Where were we? Oh yes, we had just launched ourselves into the so forth. At precisely 0837 we reached the southeast corner of the yard fence, and there we executed a smooth ninety-degree turn to the leeward larbor—or "to the left" for those not familiar with all our terminal technology.

Our *technical terminology*, let us say. I know this is pretty complicated, but just hang on and bear with me.

Oh, and let me point out that making our ninety-degree turn wasn't as easy as you might think. Do you know why? Because at the moment we executed the turn, the outside temperature on the ranch stood at only forty-five degrees. As you can see, this left us forty-five degrees short of the desired turning ratio and . . .

Let's skip the math and mush on.

We executed a perfect ninety-degree turn, and never mind all the complex calculations we had to do to pull it off, and went streaking northward up the gravel road in front of the house. At precisely 0839 I broke radio silence.

"Drover, we will now shift into our code names. Baloney Ring, this is Buttermilk Sky. Clean up the formation. You're lagging behind, over."

"Well, I'm running as fast as I can."

"That's a rodge, Ring."

"What's a rodge ring?"

"A *rodge*. It's short for roger, and I've shortened your code name from Baloney Ring to Ring. When we're airborne, we have to do these things, over."

"I'll be derned. And what's your name again?"

"Buttermilk Sky, but you can just call me Sky. It'll save us a little time."

"Boy, I sure like buttermilk."

"Rodge, Ring. Stay alert for Charlie."

"Charlie or Murphy?"

"Roger."

"*Three spies!* Oh my gosh!"

I felt my temper rising. "Drover, if this too complicated, just skip it. Stay off the radio and pay attention to—holy smokes, Drover, do you see what I see?"

"I thought I was Ringworm."

"Roger, Ringworm! Straight in front of us. Do you see it now?"

There was a moment of silence. Then Drover

23

said, "Oh. I'll be derned. It's the mail truck."

"Mail truck! Are you crazy? That's no mail truck, son. Stay in formation. We're going in for a closer—"

Huh?

Okay, what we had here was . . . tell you what, we're going to call off the Red Alert and go back to Condition Normal. It seems that we had just intercepted the . . . uh . . . mail truck, so to speak, but let me hasten to point out that the mailman was running *two whole hours* ahead of his normal schedule. He wasn't supposed to come by our ranch until 10:30, and how's a dog supposed to . . .

He hadn't bothered to notify ME of this, and it's very hard to run a ranch when they don't . . .

But the important thing is that our systems had picked up the sounds of his vehicle and we had conducted a successful test of the Scramble All Dogs Procedure. Pretty amazing, huh? You bet. I mean, we don't expect trouble from postal employees, but it never hurts to check these things out. With a dangerous spy running loose on the ranch, a dog can never be sure . . .

But wait, hold everything. Maybe there was more to this.

We've mentioned that the mailman had changed his routine, right? But what you didn't notice was that *he didn't stop at the mailbox* on the county road! Okay, maybe you weren't there and couldn't have picked up this important clue, but I noticed it right away, and all at once it seemed pretty derned suspicious.

See, he didn't stop at the mailbox, open the little door, or slide the mail into the box. He always did that, but this time—holy smokes, he was driving toward the house! What was the deal? Right away, I got on the radio.

"Onion Ring, this is Milktoast. This guy's up to something. We will now go into Escort Formation and follow him down to the house. Keep your eyes peeled."

"How do you peel your eyes?"

"Drover, please try to be serious. If you don't know how to peel your eyes, just keep them open."

"Oh, okay. I can handle that."

"Let's move out!"

And with that, we reversed our thruster engines and fell into formation beside the mail truck as it drove toward the house. Drover took the west side and I took the east. On my side, I trotted right up to the door and gave the mailman a couple of barks, just to let him know that we dogs were on the job and watching his every move.

He glared back at me through the window glass,

curled his lip, and muttered words I couldn't hear. Maybe he didn't enjoy being barked and escorted through our ranch, but that was too bad. I mean, if these people think they can just drive through the ranch any time they feel like it, they're badly mistaken.

He could mutter and mumble all he wanted, I didn't care. Once he left the county road and pulled onto our private road to the house, he became My Problem, and . . .

Have we discussed this particular postal employee? Maybe so, but it's been a while. We didn't know his name, but that didn't matter. He was a big guy with dark brooding eyes, a hateful disposition, and a bulge in his left cheek.

Right cheek? No, it was the left side. His cheek bulged out because—this will shock you—because *he chewed tobacco on the job.* Yes sir, he chewed nasty tobacco.

And he rolled down his window and yelled, "Get out of the road, moron!"

Ha! Did he think he could scare me off with threats and hateful words? You know me. When they start yelling and hurling insults, it just makes me more determined than ever to give 'em the kind of barking they so richly deserve. So instead of running away with my leg between my tails, I gave him another barking, this one even louder and more ferocious.

Furthermore, I got on the radio and ordered Drover to do the same on the other side. Heh heh. That would teach this smartypants mailman to . . .

You won't believe what he did—the mailman, that is. I was shocked, although maybe I shouldn't have been. I mean, he'd done this before and . . .

*He spit tobacco juice at me!* And I'm sorry to report that he was, well, a pretty good shot and scored a . . . I never did like that guy or trust him, and he deserved every bark I'd given him over the years.

"Be careful, Drover! He's taking countermeasures. If you see anything brown coming your way, you'd better duck!"

"Where's a duck?"

"No, I said . . . never mind, Drover. If you see anything brown coming your way . . ."

SPLAT!

Okay, that did it! This meant WAR! By George, if he wanted to get serious about this deal, I was prepared to . . . well, back off and put a little distance between us. I mean, I didn't see any sense in . . . but the important thing is that we kept him in sight and followed him all the way down to the house.

Yes sir, we followed him every step of the way, only now we were on guard against his child-ish . . . he stopped in front of the house. I stopped and motioned for Drover to do the same. He saw my hand signal and . . . oh brother, he waved back and yelled, "Oh, hi there!"

Sometimes I think . . . never mind.

The postman stopped in front of the house, stepped out of the truck, and reached into the back-seat of his vehicle. I saw his hind end sticking out and wondered what would happen if I rushed for-ward and . . . but, no, that would be too risky, so I hunkered down and observed him with a full array of instruments: VizRad (Visual Radar—eyes), Earatory Scanners (ears), and Sniffatory Analyzers (nose), the whole nine yards of high-tech equip-ment at the disposable of the Security Division.

We had him on our screen, fellers, and what-ever he did now would be recorded for all time.

Blinking my eyes against the stinging mist of the Toxic Tobacco Juice he had spat upon my head, I watched as he carried a large box up to the front door and knocked. A moment later the door opened and Little Alfred stepped out on the porch. The mailman said a few words to the boy, left him with the box, and returned to his vehicle—which he had left running.

That seems pretty suspicious, don't you think? I mean, why would a postal employee leave his vehicle running?

Maybe he was in a hurry. No clues there.

He climbed back into the vehicle, the mailman did, and slammed his door. At that point, I rushed out of my hiding place in the weeds and delivered a withering barrage of . . .

SPLAT! Tobacco juice.

He drove away, leaving me wounded and bleeding.

# A Pirate Comes
# Out of the House

Okay, maybe I wasn't exactly wounded and bleeding, but my pride had suffered a terrible blow.

Drover came rushing up. When he saw the brown stain upon my face and head, he—you won't believe this—he started laughing.

I turned to the dunce and melted him with a flaming glare. "Drover, it really hurts to see you making a mockery of my misfortunes. Just for that, I'm going to put three Irreverence Marks into your record."

"Oh drat."

"And another one for using naughty language on the job."

"Oh fizzlebloomers."

"There's another one! Go ahead, son, get all the poison out of your system."

"Oh . . . bonkeywhoofer."

"That's cute, Drover, and that brings you up to a grand total of six marks against your record. You want any more?"

He grinned. "No, I'm out of naughty words."

"Good. Great. Maybe you've cleansed your internal organs of all their grime and filth."

"Yeah, but you've still got tobacco juice on your face."

I glared at him. "Okay, smart guy, just for that, we'll make it seven marks! That last one is for speaking an Unauthorized Truth."

"Yeah, but . . ."

I did Dives in the Grass and wiped the gunk off my face and head. "And let that be a lesson to you. When I want to know the truth about my appearance, I'll let you know."

"Yeah, but . . ."

"Go to your room. Immediately!"

"Yeah, but . . . that spy's down there with the turkeys, and I'm scared of spies."

I gave that some thought. "Hmmm. Good point. Okay, maybe sending you to your room is too harsh, but, Drover, we must do something about your . . ."

"I wonder what's in the box."

32

"Quiet. I'm not finished. We must do something to improve your—what did you just say?"

"I wonder what's in the box."

I stared into the deep emptiness of his eyes. "It's not a box. It's a spy, a very dangerous spy."

"Yeah, but . . . the mailman delivered a box."

"Oh, that. Are you saying there's a spy in the box? Hurry up, Drover, what's your point?"

"I just wondered . . ." All at once, he burst out crying. "I don't know what I'm saying! You've got me so confused, I don't know if I'm coming or going!"

I heaved a sigh and patted the little mutt on the shoulder. "Try to control yourself, son. I think I can help."

33

He stopped crying and stared at me with tear-shimmering eyes. "Really? No fooling?"

"Yes. Here's the answer you've been seeking all these years, and I hope you'll pay close attention." I leaned down and whispered, "The reason you can't tell if you're coming or going is that you're going insane, and I've seen it coming for a long time."

He gave me a silly grin. "Oh. Is that all? Gosh, thanks. I feel better already."

I held him in my gaze for a long minute, as he grinned and hopped around in circles. He seemed as happy as a little bird in a birdbath. Sometimes I wonder . . . oh well.

"That's enough, Drover. We need to find out what's in that mysterious box."

And with that, we left Drover's personal problems and went streaking over to the yard gate. There, we set up a Forward Position and began monitoring the sounds and so forths that were coming from the porch.

Little did we know or even suspect—but we mustn't get the horse in front of the donkey.

We listened and watched, is the point. Little Alfred was busy, tearing at the paper that was wrapped around the box and in which the box was wrapped. Alfred was good at this sort of thing—tearing and wrecking. And you could tell that he loved his work. His eyes were sparkling.

Just then, the door opened and out stepped—oops—out stepped his mother. Sally May. And all at once I felt myself consumed with . . . well, uncomfortable feelings. A wooden smile came to my lips, I cut my eyes from side to side, and my tail . . . well, it started tapping on the ground, almost as though it had a mind of its own.

Do you see what she does to me? There I was, a model of perfect dog behavior . . . a sincere dog, a dog who did his job and tended to his business, a dog who had done nothing wrong and who had never even thought about doing anything wrong, and yet . . .

When she came onto the scene, I began to fidget and grovel and grin, and suddenly I felt consumed by terrible feelings of guilt, almost as though . . .

She saw us there at the gate, but I knew she wasn't looking at Drover. She was looking at ME—looking *at* me, *into* me, *through* me with those . . . those heartless eyes of hers, the eyes that see into the souls of dogs and little boys and always find . . . NAUGHTY THOUGHTS.

And the crazy thing was that I didn't *have* any naughty thoughts! Hey, I'd just gotten out of bed. I hadn't done anything yet. I hadn't even thought about—okay, maybe I'd barked at the mailman, but that was part of my job, right? But other than that, I was as innocent as the driveled snow.

But that didn't matter. Her eyes walked into the house of my soul and began . . . looking under the beds, lifting the lids on all the cooking pots, peering into the closets of my mind . . . and suddenly I was squirming with horrible feelings of GUILT.

In the glare of her eyes, I squirmed and fidgeted and tapped my tail and squeezed up a desperate smile which said, "Hey, Sally May, I can explain everything. It wasn't me. I didn't do it. Honest. No kidding."

Whew! It must have worked, because at last she let me off the forks of her gaze and looked down at Little Alfred. Only then did I dare relax.

"What is it, sweetie?" she asked.

Alfred was still ripping his way through the paper. "It's my costume! It finally came."

Sally May smiled. "Let's take it inside. I don't want those papers blowing all over the yard."

They went inside. I heaved a huge sigh of relief and noticed that Drover was staring at me.

"Why are you staring at me in that tone of voice?"

"Well . . . you were acting kind of funny."

"For your information, Drover, I wasn't acting, and it wasn't funny. Perhaps you weren't paying

36

attention and didn't notice that Sally May was frisking me with her eyes."

"I'll be derned. I feel kind of frisky myself. I guess it's this nice fall weather."

I glared at him. "Drover, it's not fall. It's May. It's spring."

"I'll be derned. I guess I'm not as frisky as I thought." He yawned. "In fact, I'd kind of like to take a little nap."

"Sorry, no naps. You might recall that we're in the middle of an investigation. Were you listening when Little Alfred said what was inside that mysterious box? Did you hear what it contained?"

He rolled his eyes around. "Well, let's see here. A costume?"

"Exactly. Now put the clues together."

"Okay, here we go. Box. Costume." His eyes popped open. "Oh my gosh, you don't reckon . . ."

"Yes, Drover, now we know where Murphy's getting his disguises. That box contains a turkey costume!"

Drover let out a gasp and shook his head. "Oh my gosh! So you think Alfred's part of Murphy's . . . I think I'm confused again."

I cut my eyes from side to side. "It is confusing, isn't it? But let me remind you, Drover, that we must have the courage to follow the evidence to its logical conclusion, no matter how ridiculous it seems to be. The final proof will come soon."

"You mean—"

"Exactly. If Little Alfred appears on the porch, dressed as a turkey, we'll know the awful truth."

Drover gasped and covered his heart with a paw. He just couldn't bring himself to face the possibility that Alfred, our little pal, might be part of a huge conspiracy that involved . . .

The door opened. Drover and I swung our eyes around, as each of us tried to prepare our respective selves for . . .

HUH?

What we saw coming out of the house wasn't Little Alfred. It wasn't even Little Alfred wearing a turkey disguise. It was . . . a *total stranger*, a man we'd never seen before! And unless I was badly mistaken—hang on, this will come as a terrible shock—he was a . . .

PIRATE!

Oh, I know what you're thinking. "It couldn't have been a pirate, not on a ranch in the Texas Panhandle. Pirates sail ships and the ranch just didn't have enough water to support a huge three-masted sailing ship. So it couldn't have been a pirate."

That's what you were thinking, right? Go ahead

and admit it. Well, you've raised a few good points, but I'm sorry to report that you're wrong. That guy was a pirate, no question about it, and Drover and I were staring, bug-eyed and terrified, at the evidence. Here, check this out.

**Evidence #1:** He was dressed in pirate clothes, including one of those funny-shaped hats that pirates wear.

**Evidence #2:** In his right hand, he carried a sword. And in fact, he was slashing the air with it.

**Evidence #3:** He had a black patch over one eye.

**Evidence #4:** Finally, and most shockingly, the guy had . . . *a wooden leg*!

Now, you add up all those clues and tell me he wasn't a pirate.

# CHAPTER FIVE

# Attacked by a Whole Gang of Pirates

It was one of the spookiest, scariest things I'd seen in my entire career, and I'm sorry that I can't reveal any more information about it. I absolutely can't. Wild horseflies couldn't drag it out of me.

Do you know why? *Because of the kids.* You know where I stand on the issue of scaring the kids, right? I don't mind giving 'em a little scare now and then, but when we get into the darker, really scary stuff . . . I just can't bring myself to do it.

It could have a bad effect, cause the kids to have nightmares in the night and even wet the bed. We don't need that. I mean, this world is wet enough without . . .

What? You think you can handle the scary part? You think you're tough enough?

Yeah, but what if you're wrong? What happens then? Who's going to take the blame if you wake up screaming in the night and find a wet spot on your sheets?

Okay, tell you what. I'll go on with this, but if you get in trouble, don't blame me. I've got enough problems of my own without . . .

I guess we'll find out. Hang on, here it comes.

Drover and I were so shocked, neither of us could speak nor move. We just sat there, frozen in our tracks, staring at this horrible pirate that had come slouching out of the house.

And then we heard him speak. Here's what he said, word for word. "All wight, you squids, waise the mainsail! We sail for Hispaniola on the morning tide!"

See? What did I tell you? The guy was a pirate, no question about it, and . . . well, have we discussed my Position on Pirates? Maybe not. I have no use for pirates, none at all, and I go out of my way to avoid them whenever possible.

I mean, what kind of person wears a patch over his eye, walks on a wooden leg, and goes around swinging a sword? That's exactly the kind of guy I've always wanted to avoid, so it should come as no surprise that I . . . that Drover . . . that we . . .

For a moment I was frozen by the sheer terror of

the moment. I heard a gurgling sound in my throat-alary region—a growl that was trying to make its way out of the dark dungeon of my . . . something. And then, in the eerie silence, I heard the sound of . . . uh . . . running water, and I realized . . .

"Run, Drover, run for your life!"

I needn't have bothered telling my nincompoop assistant to run. He was already gone, I mean, he'd vanished in a flash of white and a cloud of dust. The little—I don't know how he does that.

And so it was that, with the pirate's haunting laughter in my ears, I went to Turbo Five, launched all dogs into the morning breeze, and got the heck out of there.

I went roaring around the south side of the yard, bending that big cottonwood tree almost to the ground in the wake of my rocket engines, and set a Speed Course for the gas tanks. Up ahead, I caught a glimpse of something four-legged and furry walking across my path.

"Out of the way, Pete! I can't stop this thing!"

By making a few quick adjustments in my Trajectory Program, I was able to, heh heh, bull-doze our local cat and send him rolling across the gravel drive. Heh heh.

Don't get me wrong. I was much too busy to waste time wrecking cats, but . . . well, on the other hand, opportunity knocks but once, and when it knocks, a guy should . . . do something.

Answer the door.

Run over the nearest cat.

The point is that a dog should never get so busy and preoccupied with the Big Picture that he passes up a chance to bulldoze a cat. Especially Pete. If it had been any other cat, maybe I would have tried to avoid him, but since it was Pete . . .

Heh, heh.

I loved it!

But rolling up Pete into a little furry ball and causing him to hiss and yowl was just a momentary pleasure, and it did nothing to change the terribleness and seriousness of my situation. I blew past Kitty Kitty, streaked up the hill, and made a safe landing in front of the Security Division's Vast Office Complex.

There, I switched off the Rocket Dog Program, cut all engines, darted into the building, and took the elevator up to our office on the twelfth floor.

Maybe you find it hard to believe that our gas-tank office had twelve floors, and . . . okay, maybe it didn't, but nobody's impressed when you tell 'em that your office is nothing but a couple of gunny-sacks beneath the gas tanks.

On the other hand, if you tell 'em "I rode the

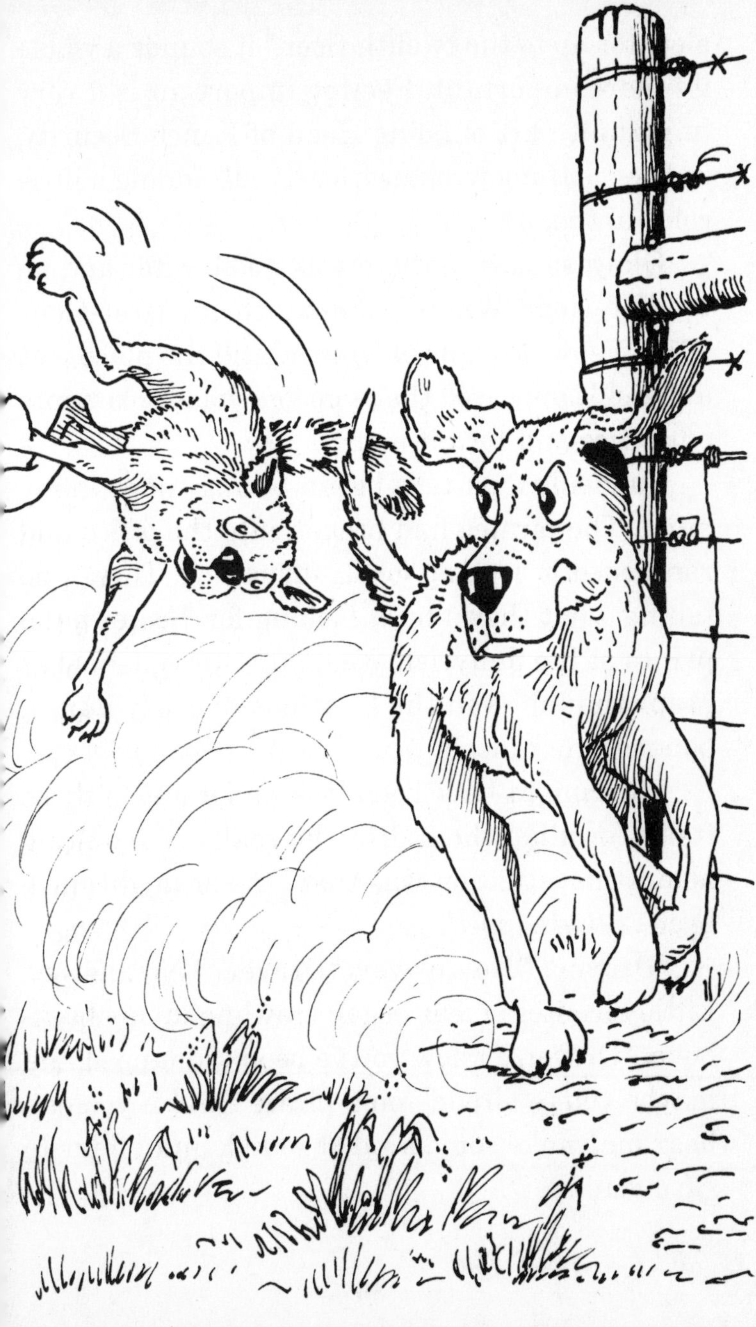

elevator up to the twelfth floor," it sounds a whole lot more important. Feeling important is a very important part of being Head of Ranch Security, so I see nothing wrong with . . . well, adding a little color to the, uh . . .

Okay, so maybe there was no elevator and no twelfth floor. When I burst into our first-floor office, I saw no signs of Drover. And the place was a mess! It appeared that someone had broken into our office and torn it apart!

Suddenly a pattern began taking shape in my mind. The pirates had broken into the office and ransacked it, looking for . . . something. There's no telling what they'd been looking for. Secret blueprints of the Jellyfish Weapon? Our codebooks? Maps that showed the locations of every buried bone on the ranch?

They might have been looking for any of those items, or all of them. But the really scary thing about this situation was that Drover might have been . . . *kidnapped*!

"Drover?" No answer. "Drover?" No answer. Little termites of fear began crawling up my backbone. "Drover, I know you've been kidnapped and maybe you're already on a pirate ship! If you can hear me, make some kind of sound, and I'll try to save you!"

In the eerie silence, I cocked my ear and listened. At first . . . nothing. Then . . . in the far, far distance, I heard a tiny voice: "Help!"

It was Drover, and yes, my worst fears were confumed. Confused. *Confirmed*.

My worse fears were confumed. He'd been kidnapped by a gang of blurdthusty pirates—bloodthirsty pirates, I should say—and now . . .

"Drover, listen carefully. Continue emitting sounds and I'll try to find you. Be brave, son. If it takes all day, I'll find you! If it takes all week— well, I'll probably give up, so hurry!"

"Help!"

"Good! I'm on the trail now. Again."

"Help!"

"That's right, good, fine. I feel I'm getting closer. One more time."

"Help!"

Using all my instruments, I locked in on the sound and followed it to the source, until at last I saw . . . his stub tail sticking out from beneath his gunnysack. I heaved a huge sigh of relief.

"Thank goodness! There you are, and Drover, I'm proud to report that you weren't kidnapped after all."

"Help!"

I kicked him on the bohunkus. "Hey! I've found

you. You're safe. You can come out now."

The sack wiggled and I saw one big eye peeking out. "Is that you, Hank?"

"Of course it's me. Against incredible odds, I tracked you down and found you. Come out, we have many things to discuss and very little time."

Drover poked his nose out from under the gunny sack and glanced around. "Hank, that was the scariest pirate I ever saw! What was he doing in the house?"

I glanced over both shoulders, just to be sure we weren't being watched. "I'm not sure, Drover, but we must prepare ourselves for the worst. It's possible that they've captured the house."

Drover gasped. "*They!* Oh my gosh! You mean..."

"Yes, Drover. They've stormed the house and taken captives. At this very moment, Sally May and Little Alfred are probably tied and gagged."

Drover vanished beneath the gunnysack. "Oh my gosh! I think I'll stay in here!"

I seized a corner of the sack in my enormous jaws and gave it a jerk, exposing a quivering white ball of dog hair. Drover. "Come out at once, and that's a direct order."

He glanced around and sat up. "Where are the pirates?"

"We're not sure, but it's obvious that they ran-sacked the office. Look at this place! It's a mess."

"Yeah, but it's always a mess. I guess we're just messy dogs."

"We don't have time to argue." I began pacing, as I often do when my mind is racing. "We'll have to assume the worst, Drover. They've stolen all our cipher books, so we'll have to change our codes and give you a whole new code name. From now on, you're no longer Buckwheat."

"I thought I was Ringworm."

"Your new code name is Jitterbug, and I'll be Laughing Gravy. How about that?"

He laughed.

"Drover, that's not funny."

"Oops, sorry. I just thought . . ."

"Please don't think. Just listen." I resumed my pacing. "They've stolen all our classified material, so we must assume that they know *everything*. They've got our battle plans, codes, blueprints—they know all our secrets, Drover."

He let out a moan. "Oh no! Do you reckon they know about . . . my leg?"

I stopped pacing and studied the runt. "Your leg? What about your leg?"

"It's my deepest, darkest secret, and I've kept it hidden all these years!"

"Yes, yes? Go on. We must know the extent of the damage."

He was almost in tears. "Well . . . okay. All these years I've had this deep, dark secret . . ."

"Drover, please get to the point."

He took a deep breath, and then blurted out, "There's nothing wrong with . . ."

Drover wasn't able to finish his sentence. At that very moment, I heard a sound off to my left . . . right . . . I heard a sound, is the point. I whirled around and saw . . .

It was worse than I could have imagined. It was awful. It made every hair on my backbone stand straight up.

And it wasn't a turkey.

# CHAPTER SIX

# We Run
# for Our Lives!

Creeping toward the gas tanks was the biggest, bloodest-thirsty pirate I'd ever seen! He was hobbling along on his wooden leg, staring at us with his one good eye, grinning an evil grin, and waving his sword. Holy smokes, he was coming to get us!

Did pirates eat dogs? I'd never heard of such a thing, but . . .

Can you take anymore of this? I'm not sure I can. I mean, I was there, I lived it, I saw it all with my very own eyes, but I'm not sure I can bear to tell about it. And don't forget about all the little children who might be listening and watching.

What do you think? We could quit this story and go to another one. I've got many other stories,

51

and they're not nearly as scary and terrifying as this one.

Keep going? Okay, you asked for this.

There we were, scared out of our wits and livers. I managed to fire off one squeak of bark, in hopes it might slow down the pirate, and then I shifted into gear and highballed it out of there.

"To the machine shed, Drover! The cowboys are up there and maybe they can save us!"

Fellers, we ran for our lives! If we could make it to the machine shed, maybe our cowboy pals could fight off this horrible villain. I mean, they had hammers and stuff in there, and maybe if all four of us mounted a defense, we could . . .

Holy smokes, I could hear the pirate's blood-chilling laughter behind us! And even worse, when I dared to throw a glance over my shoulder, I saw that . . . he was coming after us! I could even hear his wooden leg thumping on the ground!

"Faster, Drover! He's coming!"

The little mutt was pumping his legs as fast as they would go. "Help! Murder! My leg's killing me! Oh, the pain!"

Drover had practically confessed that there was nothing wrong with his leg, and yet—well, we sure as thunder didn't have time to stop and discuss his so-called bad leg.

We went streaking all the way up the hill and didn't slow down until we saw the machine shed up ahead. There, we went to Full Air Brakes, slid right up to the big double doors, and dived inside.

Lucky for us, Slim and Loper were there, doing some shop work—clanging, banging, welding, yelling, grinding—doing all the things they have to do to keep the machinery running. Slim was under the welding hood, kneeling on the floor and welding on a piece of metal. Maybe I should have barked a warning, but there wasn't time, and besides I was out of breath, so I had no choice but to . . .

The back of his shirt had come untucked, don't you see, and all at once it occurred to me that . . . well, it resembled a tent, a nice cozy tent. Maybe there'd be room inside his tent for . . . ME, you might say. Why not? We'd been pals for many years. We'd slept in the same bed, eaten off the same plate, ridden in the same pickup, shared many adventures together, so it seemed perfectly natural, perfectly reasonable that . . .

I mean, if Slim had known that I was being chased by a wild, screeching, dog-eating pirate, I'm almost sure that he would have wanted me to jump inside his shirt. In fact, he would have *demanded* it.

That's the kind of friendship we had—tested by fire and time, true to the bone.

I knew it would be a tight squeeze, but I had a feeling that I could do it. I dashed up behind him and in a flash . . .

It was lousy luck that I'd forgotten about my nose. A dog's nose, by its very nature, is wet and cold, right? And, okay, Slim was under the welding hood and didn't even know I was around, so . . . uh . . . when my cold nose came into contact with his bare skin . . .

"YEEEE-OW!"

Gee whiz, I'd never suspected that Slim could move so fast or jump so high. I mean, welding rods and cords and slag hammers went flying in all directions, and so did the welding hood. When his feet came back to Mother Earth, he whirled around and—gosh, his eyes were flaming.

I knew at once that this incident was going to . . . uh . . . put a strain on our friendship, so right away I switched over to Looks of Remorse and Tragic Wags in the tail section. A lot of times that'll turn a bad situation around, don't you know, especially if we put our hearts and souls into the presentation.

That's what I did, and also squeezed up a little smile that said, "Oh. Slim. Were you inside that

shirt? I . . . uh . . . had no idea . . . look, I can explain everything. A pirate was trying to eat me."

He leveled a finger at me and said, "Hank, if you ever cold-nose me again . . ."

He wasn't able to finish his threat, because at that very moment, the dreaded pirate appeared at the door of the shed.

His one horrible, bloodshot eye looked straight at me. My gaze was locked on him. He uttered a chilling laugh, and I tried to growl back but . . . well, it came out sounding like something else. A gurgle or a yodel. It wasn't my usual manly growl, but what's a guy to do?

I kept waiting for Slim and Loper to respond to this emergency. I mean, here was a notorious pirate, walking right into our machine shed, and Slim and Loper were just . . . you know what they did? They were watching the whole thing and *grinning*!

Hey, what about fighting him off with hammers and clubs? What about rushing to the aid of the Head of Ranch Security? What about lending a hand to defend the ranch against—

He lurched another step in my direction, the pirate did, and his sword ripped through the air. Okay, that did it. It was clear by then that I would get no help from my so-called cowboy friends, so I was forced to go to Drastic Measures.

I did what any normal red-blooded American dog would have done. I turned toward the north wall of the shed and prepared to blow a hole right through the middle of it! Yes sir, if nobody was going to help me, I would have to help myself.

The trick to knocking down walls and blowing holes in the sides of barns is *acceleration*. If a dog can go from a standing start to the speed of light in just a matter of seconds, he can . . . BONK! . . . ruin his nose and knock himself silly, without making the slightest impression on the stupid wall.

As I lay there, flat on my back, staring up at the mud dauber nests on the ceiling joists, I heard . . . laughter. The laughter of two overgrown children who pretended to be cowboys, and who were always quick to laugh at the misfortunes of others.

Slim and Loper.

One of them said, "Alfred, you scared that poor dog half to death. Where'd you get the pirate suit?"

HUH?

Alfred? Pirate suit?

I staggered to my feet, just in time to see—you won't believe this.

Okay, we can call off the Code Three. You thought we'd been attacked by a notorious pirate? Ha ha. Not at all, and I'd never been totally . . .

this will come as a huge shock, but I can now reveal that the pirate was actually . . . Little Alfred.

Ha ha. No problem, no big deal.

See, the boy and his dad had been staying up late at night, reading *Treasure Island*, a book about . . . well, pirates and stuff. And Sally May had ordered Alfred a pirate costume out of a catalog, so that he could play . . . what was the name of the guy?

High Ho Silver?

Gung Ho Silver?

Some guy named Silver, a pirate with a wooden leg and . . . Hong Kong Silver? . . . and a patch over his eye, and I guess he went around waving his sword all the time . . . King Kong Silver? . . . and scaring people and dogs. Anyway, you get the picture. Alfred had put on his costume and had come out on the porch to see if he could . . . well, terrify his doggies, I suppose, but he hadn't fooled me, not even for a . . .

Okay, he'd fooled me for just a little while, but as far as me believing that we actually had a real live pirate on the ranch . . . ha ha . . .

Long John Silver. There we go.

So what we had here was just a simple case of mistaken . . . although I must admit that my feelings were pretty badly damaged over the deal. I'd always known that Slim and Loper were shameless jokers, but what really broke my heart about this deal was that their childish ways had rubbed off on Little Alfred.

And now that the scary part was over, I realized that Alfred needed to be *shunned*.

With my nose throbbing and my eyes still watering from the wall experience, I held my head at a proud angle and marched out of the shed, past the jeering masses and the tiny minds who had nothing better to do than to goof off and make jokes.

As I passed Alfred, I beamed him a sad look that said, "Well, this is the end of a long friendship and a glorious career. You leave me with no choice, Alfred. I'm resigning my position with the Security Division and quitting in disgrace. When the sun goes down tonight, I'll be gone. Good-bye."

It was a tragic moment, one of the darkest moments of my entire career. Not only had I lost my home and ranch, but they had lost . . . ME.

# CHAPTER SEVEN

# The Bubble-Gum Adventure

Outside the shed, it was my misfortune to encounter Drover. Where had he been through my terrible ordeal, and how had he gotten outside? I had no idea. Furthermore, I didn't care.

"Hank, did you hear that loud crash?"

"Not only did I hear that loud crash, I *was* that loud crash. Good-bye, Drover."

"I'll be derned. Hey, wait a minute."

I stopped and looked down at the mutt. "Yes? Be brief. I've been shamed and disgraced, and I'll be leaving soon."

"Yeah, but...we didn't solve the case of Murphy the Spy. That pirate was Little Alfred."

"So it seems, Drover. I was wrong and I made

a fool of myself. Well, they got their laughs out of me, and now I'm leaving."

His eyes grew wide. "Leaving! You mean—"

"Yes, Drover. I'm quitting, resigning my position. I no longer care about the Murphy Case or the Pirate Invasion. Let some other dog have all the worry and responsibility."

"Yeah, but . . ."

Just then, Little Alfred came out of the shed. He was smiling. "Hankie, did I scare you wiff my costume?"

I turned my eyes away.

"Well, don't be mad. I was just having some fun."

Don't be mad? Ha!

He put his arm around me and patted me on the ribs. "We can still be fwiends, can't we? Maybe we can pway Tweasure Island."

Play? Ha! No, my feelings had been shattered beyond all repair, and so had our friendship.

"I might give you a tweat."

A treat? No thanks, pal. Things had gone too far, and I couldn't be bribed.

The boy looked up at the sky. "What if I gave you . . . my bubble gum?"

Nope, wouldn't work. The damage was just too great, and—well, I'd never tried bubble gum and probably wouldn't like it. No.

He reached into his mouth and brought out a gooey wad of something pink. "It's pwetty good."

It probably was "pwetty good," but dogs didn't chew . . .

He held it under my . . . sniff, sniff . . . nose, and you know what? It did smell pretty good, I mean, *real good*, but as far as me being bribed by a piece of . . .

I don't know how this happened, but suddenly my tongue . . . well, somehow it shot out of my mouth and made contact, shall we say, with the . . .

My eyes brightened. My ears shot up. *That* was bubble gum?

He grinned. "What do you think?"

I thought . . . you know, time heals all wounds, even the terrible wounds of the spirit, and quite a bit of time had passed . . . and I was feeling a whole lot better about my . . . uh . . . okay, what the heck. I would accept his offer, and yes, I might even consider sticking around and playing pirates with him.

I took his peace offering into my mouth and began chewing it up. Hey, this stuff was great!

Alfred beamed a smile. "And now we're fwiends again, aren't we?"

Oh yes! The best of friends, no question about it.

"Okay, Hankie. We're gonna make us a ship in

a twee. Come on." Alfred started walking off to the south.

Right, you bet, no problem. What a fine lad! Yes, maybe he had fallen under the corrupting influence of the local cowboys, but I wasn't the kind of dog who held a grudge. I mean, true friends forgive and . . .

I shewed and shewed on that bubblygum. It was 'licious, great shuff, but I couldn't get it shewed op.

But back to the bishnesh of friendship . . . I've always shed that any friendship worth having ish worth . . .

*Gorp, gop, slurp.*

You know, the wonger I shewed that schtuff, the bigger it got, and it wuss schtarting to gummup my cheeth . . .

Suddenly I realized that Drover was staring at me. "Boy, I sure wish I had some bubble gum. Is it pretty good? I ate some one time, and the longer I chewed, the bigger it got. It sure did gum up my teeth."

I gave him a withering glare and said, *"Glop glork glum slum slop."*

Hey, this was getting serious! I couldn't chew it up, I couldn't swallow it, I couldn't spit it out. I tried everything. I moved my jaws, I moved my

tongue, I pawed at my mouth, I ran in circles . . .
yipes, that stuff had gotten hold of me and I
couldn't . . .

Just then, when I was nearing the point of
desperation, Slim stepped outside and saw that I
was in an emergency situation. Shaking his head,
he came over to me.

"Hank, what's got hold of you?" He pried open
my jaws and pulled out the stringy gob of gooey
yucko gum. "Oh, I see. Birdbrain. There. Now, next
time you get a chance to . . ."

He held the gum between his right thumb and
forefinger, then tried to remove it with his left
thumb and forefinger. He merely pulled it into two
pieces, with a long thread of gum hanging between
them. He gave both hands a shake, but the stuff
didn't come off. He tried to rub it off on the ground,
but that didn't work either. The gum was now
clinging to both hands, and he had pink threads of
it on his boots, shirt, and glasses. There was dirt
stuck all over it.

He looked at me and sighed. "Well, I guess it
serves me right for laughing at you, huh pooch?"

That was exactly right, which just goes to prove
that Justice has a way of chasing us down, no matter how hard we laugh or try to escape it.

I gave Slim one last smirk and marched away,

leaving him with the problem of how to get out of my Bubble-Gum Trap.

See, I'd planned it this way all along. No kidding. After he had made such a joke out of my misfortune, I had plotted a way of getting my revenge, and he had walked right into my clever trap. No kidding. And it served him right.

Anyway, Alfred and Drover had walked down the hill, and I joined them. Alfred had plopped down on the ground and was in the process of removing his—oh, so that was it! You remember that business of the wooden leg? It wasn't real, just a thing made out of plastic. He had doubled up his left leg, see, and tied the thing on with leather straps.

I had, uh, noticed that right away, the very minute he'd walked out on the porch. Honest.

"It's too much twouble," he explained. "And besides, you can't cwimb a twee wiff a wooden weg."

Well, yes, that made sense. But why did he need to climb a tree? I mean, why would a pirate . . .

I soon found out, and it turned out to be a pretty good idea. See, he borrowed an old sheet from his momma, climbed up into a tree, and tied the sheet to a couple of tree limbs, making a sail. Up in a fork of the tree, Alfred's dad had nailed some one-by-six-foot boards to the limbs, giving us a "deck." And suddenly we had ourselves a real, genuine sailing ship! Pretty slick, huh?

That done, he turned a stern gaze on me and Drover. "Okay, doggies, we're fixing to sail our ship, and we're gonna find some buried tweasure!"

Buried treasure, huh? Hey, this was sounding better and better.

"Hank, you can be Jim Hawkins." I saluted the captain and thumped my tail on the ground. "And Dwover, you can be . . . Billy Bones."

Drover fluttered his stub tail and said, "Oh good, 'cause I sure like bones."

"And now," said Captain Long John Alfred, "our ship's weady to sail. But how can we get y'all dogs into the ship?"

Hmmm. That was a problem, all right, because . . . well, dogs don't climb trees. Or ships. We're not climbers, don't you see.

The captain thought about it for a long minute, and then he came up with an idea. He told Dwover and me to wait right there— Drover and me, that is—whilst he went to gather up some equipment. He returned ten minutes later with . . . my goodness, a length of rope and a five gallon bucket. He tied one end of the wope . . . uh, rope . . . to the handle of the bucket and . . .

Wait a minute, hold everything. He thought I was going to climb into the bucket so that he could haul me—ha ha. No thanks, pal. There are many things a loyal dog will do for his friends, but as far as me . . .

Sniff, sniff. My goodness, something inside the bucket smelled . . . sniff, sniff . . . pretty good. I, uh, felt it was my duty to stick my head into the bucket to check this out . . .

"No, no, Hankie. My mom made some sandwiches and that's our food for the twip. We can't eat 'til we get on the ship and set sail. I'll take the food up first, then pull you up."

Oh, so that was it. Okay, sure, fine. Food for the trip. Great idea, and he sure didn't need to worry about me . . . sniff, sniff. Unless I was badly mistaken, there were two fat tuna fish sandwiches in there!

Have we discussed tuna fish sandwiches? Maybe not, so here's my Position on Tuna Fish. Slim eats tuna fish right out of the can, and if you ask me tuna out of the can tends to be either too dry or too greasy. I'm not crazy about Slim's tuna fish. But Sally May . . .

Sally May makes the best tuna fish sandwiches in the whole world, and her trick is that she adds a bunch of stuff to the tuna: mayonnaise, sweet pickles, chopped-up boiled egg. And you know what else? She even goes to the trouble of putting a crisp leaf of lettuce on it!

No kidding, what she does to an ordinary tuna fish sandwich is amazing. It's the sort of thing only a mother would do, the sort of thing a bachelor cowboy would never do, not even in a thousand . . .

Sniff, sniff.

"Hankie, get your nose away fwom my food!"

Huh?

Me? Hey, he sure didn't need to worry about . . . in fact, I would stand right there and *guard* it for him! That's the kind of dog I was, loyal to the . . . sniff, sniff . . . end. No kidding.

Yes, it was a good thing I was there to, uh, guard the ship's provisions, because at that very moment, Captain Alfred started climbing up the tree.

I watched as he climbed up the trunk of the big cottonwood, sniffer and sniffer . . . uh, higher and higher, I should say, and all at once it occurred to me, heh heh, that he wasn't exactly watching me like a hawk anymore, so I . . .

I found myself staring into the grinning face of a cat! Yes, it was Mister Kitty Moocher and no doubt he'd caught the scent of the tuna fish sandwiches and had come to check it out. The foolish cat even hopped up on his back legs and peered into the bucket.

I went straight into Menacing Growls. "Kitty, I wouldn't do that if I were you."

"Oh, hello, Hankie. I wonder what's inside the bucket."

"Then let me tell you. What's inside the bucket is trouble."

"Mmmm. Trouble smells good."

"Yes, Kitty, trouble often smells good. If it smelled bad, cats like you might never blunder into it. Now scram."

Pete pinned his ears down on his head and did that thing with his eyes . . . how do I describe it? I'm not sure. The center part of the eye grows bigger than normal, don't you see, and it's something cats do when they're mad or unhappy. Maybe they think it scares the opposition, and maybe it does if the opposition is an ordinary dog. Me? Ha! If Kitty wanted to scare the Head of Ranch Security, he would have to . . .

Huh?

All at once, Captain Alfred pulled on the rope and . . . hey, what was the deal here? My sandwiches started rising in the air . . . well, the bucket rose in the air, and the bucket just happened to contain . . .

In a flash, almost by magic, my tongue leaped out of my mouth and I began . . . licking my chops, shall we say, as I watched this tragedy unfoil. Unfold. I hopped up on my back legs and grabbed one last sniff of—boy, those things smelled terrific! I could even smell the boiled egg and the mayonnaise!

But then they were gone, snatched out of my grisp by our ship's captain, who hauled the bucket up into the tree.

Into the ship, our three-masted sailing vessel.

I had just missed a great opportunity to . . . uh . . . continue guarding the sandwiches, shall we say. However . . .

# CHAPTER EIGHT

# I Try to Do Business with the Cat

Captain Alfred was sitting in a fork of the tree, pulling the bucket up by the rope. When he got it all the way up, he removed the sandwiches, which were wrapped in paper napkins, and placed them on the deck, then lowered the bucket to the ground.

Pete beamed me a cunning smile. "Well, Hankie, I guess you don't get a bite."

"Hey, Pete, for your information, I was guarding those sandwiches, and it never even crossed my mind to eat them."

"Oh really? How come you were licking your chops, hmmm?"

"I wasn't licking my chops, Kitty, or if I was, it had nothing whatsoever to do with eating Alfred's lunch. Furthermore, I'm shocked and asandwiched that you'd even suggest such a tunable thing ... terrible thing. Just because you're a greedy little moocher doesn't mean that the rest of us have such corrupt minds."

His eyes widened. "Oooo! Well, maybe I was wrong, Hankie."

"Of course you were wrong. You're always wrong. You were wrong the day you were born, and you've gotten wronger ever since. Now, if you'll be kind enough to buzz off, I have many things to do. We're fixing to take a long and dangerous sea voyage on the sea—and you're not invited."

"Well, just darn the luck!" He batted his eyes and grinned. "See you around, Hankie."

As he walked away, I yelled, "Not if I see you first, you little pest!"

Drover was watching, and he was impressed. "Boy, you really got him on that one! Nice shot."

I rolled the muscles in my enormous shoulders and glared after the cat. "Yes, well, putting these cats in their place is a very important part of our job, Drover. Let a cat go a couple of days without a humbling and the next thing you know ..."

Holy smokes, it had suddenly occurred to me that Captain Alfred was coming down the tree ... climbing out of our ship, that is, and Pete was climbing *up*!

Do you see what this meant? The little sneak was heading toward MY SANDWICHES!!

Hey, this was getting serious! I couldn't just stand there and let the stupid cat . . . but dogs don't climb trees, right? Very seldom. We just weren't made for climbing trees or boarding ships, but there was Pete, inching his way up the . . .

I had to do something! Unless I took bold and immediate action, the thieving little cat was going to eat my . . . that is, he might very well steal Alfred's lunch. And you know how I am about these kids and their dietary so-forths. Growing boys need a good nourishing lunch. They need the many finnomins and minerals that are contained in . . . well, in tuna fish sandwiches, for example.

This was a moment of decision. I had to make a stand for Healthy Children! And so it was that, in a flash, I hopped myself into the five-gallon bucket, and as Captain Alfred walked up to me, I beamed him Looks of Greatest Urgency which said, "Captain, I request permission to board the ship. Haul me up, sir!"

Alfred stared at me and grinned. "Gee, what a good doggie."

Right, exactly. That was me, a good doggie to the bitter end. And, uh, we needed to hurry up, before a certain cat . . .

Alfred climbed back up into the tree. He hadn't noticed the cat, but that was okay. I would take care of the cat, heh heh, if Alfred would just hoist me up there.

The boy leaned back and started pulling on the rope. It was hard work and I could hear him grunting and straining, but he stayed with it. I rode the bucket, higher and higher, until at last I was there!

I leaped out of the bucket onto the deck and found myself standing right ... sniff, sniff ... right beside the captain of our ship, let us say. The boy was tired and breathing hard, and to show him just how proud I was, I gave him a big juicy lick on the face.

"Well done, Captain! Against incredible odds, we have ..."

It was then that I noticed ... well, the ground. The ground was a long, long way down there, and the wind had started blowing and the tree ... the ship, that is, the ship was beginning to roll on a stormy sea and ...

Yipes! Quick as a wink, I wrapped all four paws around the nearest tree limb, and suddenly it dawned on me that—*dogs don't belong in trees*! And at that very same moment, Alfred started climbing down the tree—to see if he could get

Drover to sit in the bucket, it appeared—but, hey, what about me?

"Alfred, son, don't leave me up here in this tree! Listen, this was a bad idea. In a moment of sandwich lust, I forgot that . . . Alfred, I'm scared of heights! There it is, I admit it, and if you go back down, you'll be leaving your very best and dearest friend . . ."

He didn't hear, or didn't understand my pleadings. He left me there, all alone and clinging to the swaying limb.

Oh brother! I'd really done it now. How could I have . . . and what made it even worse and more awful was that I was so busy hanging on that I couldn't even think about those sandwiches. I mean, I could smell 'em. They were right there beside me, but I didn't dare turn loose of the limb and . . .

HUH?

Pete?

Oh no! There he stood, right in front of me—grinning and purring and flicking the end of his tail back and forth. He had somehow managed to show up at the very moment of my darkest hour!

Our eyes met. In his whiny voice, Pete said, "Well, well, it's Hankie the Wonder Dog. I didn't know you liked being in trees."

"Oh yes, I hang out in trees all the time. Hey,

Pete, I guess you noticed the sandwiches, huh? Well, I've been thinking . . . maybe we can work out some kind of . . . uh . . . deal. Here, check this out. You take one sandwich and I'll take the other. Fifty-fifty split, fair and square. What do you say?"

He looked me over, and I had a feeling that he noticed . . . well, that I was clinging to the limb for dear life. "Pete, I wouldn't make such a generous offer to any other cat, but . . . what the heck, we've known each other for years, right? And I've always kind of liked you, and I've always thought we ought to . . . uh . . . do some business together."

Pete pushed his nose inside the wrapper on one of the sandwiches. His eyes grew wide. "Well, that's very nice, Hankie. Let me take a bite and then we'll talk deal."

"Good idea, Pete. Sure. Take your time."

I must tell you that it was *killing me* to talk nice to the cat! Before my very eyes, he took a bite off the sandwich and chewed it up. And all I could do was watch!

Meanwhile, down on the ground, Captain Alfred was trying to poke Drover into the bucket, but he was having no luck at all. Drover, the little weenie, was scared of riding in buckets and even scareder of going up into trees.

Pete chewed up his first bite and took another

one. He beamed me a big, scheming cattish smile. "Mmmmm! Oh, Hankie, this is delicious! Have you tried it?"

"I, uh, no. Not yet. To be very frank, Pete, and I'm being perfectly honest here . . . I'm a little concerned about . . . falling out of this tree."

"Are you? Poor doggie!" He took another bite. "Oh, this is—Hankie, you would just love this sandwich!"

"I'm sure I would, you little—" I strained to keep a pleasant tone in my voice. "Here's an idea, Pete. Maybe you could . . . you know, put a bite in my mouth. Then we could share it together. Sharing Life's precious moments is very important, you know."

He gave that some thought. "No, I think I'll eat some more by myself. But maybe we could share . . ." He batted his eyes and grinned. ". . . the smell. Here."

Do you know what he did? He picked up the sandwich in his front paws and held it right under my nose! And you can imagine what that did. All at once my mouth was watering and my whole body trembled with antsipitation . . . antsiperation . . . whatever it was, my whole body trembled with it, and I just couldn't resist taking a snap . . .

Yipes! I almost fell out of the tree!

I dug in with all four sets of claws, and then had to watch the cat eat the rest of my sandwich. It was a terrible ordeal, but I still had hopes . . .

"Anyway, back to our deal, Pete. You've had a chance to sample the goods, and gosh, you're probably stuffed by now . . . ha ha . . . so, uh, what do you say?"

He yawned and stretched and took his sweet time in answering. "You know, Hankie, I'd love to do business with you, but I think maybe I'll . . . eat the other one too."

I stared at him. "What! Pete, this isn't fair. It's cheating. You're taking unfair advantage of this tragedy in my life."

He nodded. "I know, Hankie, and I just love it!"

A ferocious growl was trying to work its way up my throatalary region, and I had to stomp it down with Iron Discipline. See, I still had some hope of working out a deal with the swindling little . . . I showed him a pleasant face.

"Okay, I hear you, Pete, and I think I have the answer. Check this out. We'll throw out the old deal and cut a new one—with a better split for you. Instead of fifty-fifty, we'll go . . . say, seventy-five–twenty-five. I mean, you've worked hard, you deserve it. What do you say?"

I held my breath and watched as he licked his

left front paw with a long pink tongue. "Well, Hankie, that's a pretty good offer."

"See? What did I tell you? Okay, if you'll just . . ."

"But I like my deal better. I think I'll eat the other sandwich . . . but *you can watch*."

Huh?

Right there before my very eyes, the little thief took a huge, gluttonous bite out of . . .

Okay, that did it! A dog can stand only so much. I had tried to be reasonable, I'd made him the most generous offer a dog could make, and now I had to listen to him smacking and slurping, and . . .

Something snapped inside my head.

Suddenly I forgot that I was scared of heights and that dogs don't climb around in trees. Fellers, a terrible injustice had been done and I was fixing to teach this cat a lesson I wouldn't soon forget!

# CHAPTER NINE

# Help!

It was pretty amazing. All at once I lost all fear and had but one blazing thought in my mind: *Pete would pay for this*!

I loosened my grip on the limb and planted my feet firmly on the deck. I stood up to my full height of massiveness. Then I raised my lips, revealing two rows of deadly fangs, and a huge rumble of righteous growling thundered in the depths of my throat.

The cat stared up at me with terror-stroken eyes. "Now, Hankie, don't be angry."

"Ha! It's too late for that, Kitty. You've pushed me over the edge. You didn't like my first or second deal? Okay, pal, try this one!"

I jumped right into the middle of him. I mean, I had the little snot buried under an avalanche of . . . you know, a guy forgets what cats do when you jump in the middle of 'em. They turn into a buzz saw, is more or less what they do, and before I knew it, the miserable, whiny little creep had . . . well, chainsawed my face, shall we say.

But that was okay, it was a small price to pay for the major victory I was fixing to win, if I could just get my paws on the little . . . through watering eyes, I armed all bombs and made another dive at him.

He ran, of course. Your cowards and your cats always run, but running wouldn't save Pete this time. He scampered out onto a limb, and you should have seen the fear in his eyes! He was shocked, stunned, astoopered, and do you know why? *Because I followed him.*

The dumb cat! He thought I was scared of heights, scared of trees, and that I couldn't follow a rinkydink little cat all the way out to . . .

HUH?

The limb seemed to be . . . uh . . . bending under my enormous . . . and all of a sudden I found myself way out on the end of . . .

I went to Total Lockdown and hugged the limb with all four paws. Unless I was badly mistaken, I had just . . . I saw the ground five hundred feet below me . . . a thousand feet . . . two miles below me. Alfred was staring up at me with wide eyes, and he looked about the size of an ant.

Uh-oh. Fellers, we had big problems here, and all at once pounding the cat seemed quite a bit less important than . . . in desperation, I initiated a program we save for emergencies just like this one. We call it "Moans and Wails."

Did it hurt my pride to do Moans and Wails in front of the grinning, sniveling cat? Yes, it hurt me deeply, but under the circumstances, I had no choice. I cranked up the heavy-dutiest Moans and Wails I could muster.

Down below, I heard Captain Alfred gasp. "Uh-oh, Hankie's in twouble. I'd better go get my dad!"

What a fine lad! He took off running to the machine shed as fast as his little legs would carry him, and he even dropped his sword so that he could run faster.

So there I was, clinging for dear life to a shrimpy little tree branch. And by the way, the wind was blowing harder than ever and that shrimpy tree branch was rolling and swaying, making my situation even scarier and more depressing. Do you think Pete cared? Do you think he showed any concern or remorse? No sir. None. Zero.

What he did was . . . you won't believe this . . . the little wretch walked right over my face and strolled down my backbone. And then he turned and said,

"Well, Hankie, if you need any help . . . call the dog-catcher. Bye-bye."

"Pete, you're despicable!"

"I know, Hankie, but you make it so easy."

"You'll pay for this, Kitty! When I get out of this tree . . ."

He left! The hateful little worm just turned and walked away.

A strong gust of wind came up and the branch began rolling around in the wind like a tiny boat upon a raging sea.

"Help! Help! We've got a Code Three situation on the ranch! Send all units to the cottonwood tree at once! This is not a test! Repeat, this is not a test! Alfred, hurry up!"

I barked. I moaned. I howled. And the howler I louded, the more the tree swayed and bent in the wind, the terrible wind. I battled the raging seas and clung to my tiny life raft of a branch, moaning and howling and sending out one distress call after another.

Down on the ground, Drover was squeaking and running in circles. A lot of good that did, but at least the little mutt was sharing my pain.

Then, thank goodness, I heard voices to the north. I turned and saw Slim and Loper—do you suppose they were *running* down the hill? Oh no. They were walking, as casually as if they were . . . I mean, they were talking and laughing and taking their sweet time, while Captain Alfred (my one true pal in this crowd, it seemed) tugged at his daddy's arm, trying to get him to hurry.

I must admit that I felt a mixture of emotions about accepting help from those two jugheads. On the one hand, I sure needed help, but on the other hand, I knew that I would pay a heavy price for it. They were jokers, right? They never missed an opportunity to scoff and mock at the misfortunes of others, right?

I mean, those two could take a normal situation and make it look silly, and . . . okay, my present situation was a long way from normal and already looked pretty silly, so I had every reason to fear that they would . . .

Sure enough, they approached the tree, wearing wide grins on their faces. See? I knew it. All at once I wished that Alfred hadn't bothered—the limb swayed and rocked in a blast of wind, and I hung on for dear life.

Okay, I was ready to take whatever came my way. I just wished they would hurry up!

They were still talking, and I could hear their voices now. They were talking about . . . some guy who'd made a great bareback ride at the Pampa rodeo.

Can you believe that? What a couple of bird-brains! Hey, I was trapped and macarooned in the topmost branches of a tree, in the middle of a terrible wind storm that was tossing me around like a . . .

I cranked up a fresh round of Moans and Groans. Slim looked up. "Hank, just relax. We're in a deep intellectual discussion."

Oh, sure. Right. Deep intellectual . . . I moaned and howled. Help!

Slim shook his head. "Alfred, how did that bozo get up in a tree? I mean, the last time I checked, normal dogs don't climb trees."

Alfred did his best to explain. We'd been playing pirates and . . . so forth. Slim and Loper got several good chuckles out of that, but then Loper scratched the back of his head and said, "Well, I'm glad you're using your imagination, son, but—Slim, how are we going to get him down?"

Their smiles vanished and their laughter died, as suddenly they were thrust back into the world of normal people—the world where emergencies aren't funny and tragedies aren't a joke, the world where dogs don't climb trees for sport and cowboys have to grow up.

And all at once they were scratching their heads
and scuffing up dirt with their boots and struggling
to use their tiny brains for something constructive.
I could see the pain it brought them, and I must
admit that it caused my wicked heart to sing. No
kidding, it really did, and here's the very song my
wicked heart was singing.

## You Have to Grow Up, Boys

Well, what did you expect, you clowns
    in cowboy clothes?
Did you think that life's a comedy, a
    never-ending show?
It's not. I know that shocks you, from
    your heads down to your toes,
And now you have to face the facts that
    everybody knows (but you).

I'm really very patient, I'm trying to ignore
The thousand pranks you've pulled on me
    that hurt me to the core,
But I'll be frank, your jokes are stale and
    you've become a bore,
And your ridicule and mockery have made
    me rather sore.

You have to grow up, boys, you have
    to mature.

Your humor's as funny as chicken manure.
I know that you'll fight it as long as you can.
You have to grow up, boys, it's part of the
plan.

I guess you think it's funny that a dog has
climbed a tree.
When you looked up here and saw me,
what you said was, "Tee hee hee!
Old Hank is really working hard on ranch
security!"
And then began the laughing and the
slapping of the knee.

I really am astonished at how childish you
can sound.
Making mockeries and silly jokes while
standing on the ground.
I wish that I could charge you for your laughter
by the pound,
But here's the joke, you hammerheads—*you
have to get me down!* (Ho ho!)

You have to grow up, boys, you have to
mature.
Your humor's as funny as chicken manure.
I know that you'll fight it as long as you can.
You have to grow up, boys, it's part of the
plan.

Pretty amazing song, don't you think? You bet it was, and don't forget that I composed it under the very harshest of conditions. No ordinary dog could have done such a thing. It was just too bad the jokers couldn't hear it.

It wouldn't have changed them or done any good, but I wish they could have heard it.

Where were we? Oh yes. I was up in the tree, riding out a very dangerous Code Three Situation, and the cowboys stood down below, facing the shocking prospect that they might have to grow up and do something constructive.

Even at a distance, I could see that it was hard on them. At last Loper said, "I think I've got a plan. Alfred, go get your mother, and tell her to bring a blanket."

Alfred took off running to the house, and notice that he *ran*. He didn't walk or loiter or lollygag around like some people I could name.

By now, you're probably sitting on the edge of your chair, worried sick and wondering if they succeeded in getting me out of the tree. You'll just have to wait and see.

# CHAPTER TEN

# The Rescue Mission Fails

This is getting pretty scary, don't you think? You bet, but I hope you'll stick with me. You probably think they got me out of the tree and everything worked out just fine, but I must warn you that we're still a long way from that.

Let me set the scene again. Through circumstances beyond my control, I had gotten myself stranded in a tree, but don't forget that I wasn't sitting on a nice fat limb. That would have made everything easy.

No, thanks to Sally May's scheming, treacherous little weasel of a cat, I had been lured away from the big limbs and had crawled my way out to the end of a shrimpy little limb, which was bending under my weight and swaying in the wind.

Do you see the meaning of this? In the first place, I wasn't *about* to release my grip on that limb, because . . . well, because it was unthinkable. Hey, I was no dummy. If I let go of that limb, I would fall to the ground and would be splattered all over the ranch.

Okay, that's Point One. Point Two is that neither Slim nor Loper could reach me, because the limb would break under their respective weights.

So when we add up the evidence in this case (Point One + Point Two), we come up with Point Three (1+2=3): How could they get me out of the tree if they couldn't reach me?

That was the terrible dilemma that faced us, but you'll be relieved to know that Loper had come up with a pretty good plan of action, and here's the scoop on that. Captain Alfred returned with his momma, who carried Baby Molly in one arm and a wool blanket in the other.

Oh, and did I mention that Sally May didn't look real happy? She didn't. It appeared that she had been right in the middle of baking an angel food cake when Alfred had burst into the kitchen and called her out for Emergency Duty. She'd been forced to turn off the oven and leave the cake inside, and her first words to me were "If my cake falls . . ."

I held my breath, waiting for a long list of all

the things she would do to me. But she didn't list them. Instead, she glared up at me and muttered, "Hank, you are so dumb!"

That hurt. It really hurt. I hardly knew how to respond. I mean, I had to admit that this whole thing had the markings of something that was ... well, pretty dumb, to use her words.

But she'd responded to the call, that was the important thing, and maybe we could, uh, work out the details at a later time.

So there they were, gathered at the base of the tree, and Loper put his Rescue Plan into action. Sally May set Molly down in the grass. She opened up the blanket and each of them gripped one of the four corners. (All blankets have four corners. Did you know that? It's true).

Then they positioned themselves and the blanket right below—well, below ME, you might say, and Loper called out, "Okay, Hank. Jump!"

Jump?

Me, jump?

Was he crazy? Hey, for his information I was two thousand feet above the ground, and I had a Double Death Grip on that limb and I wasn't fixing to ...

Okay, Loper's plan suddenly became clear to me. They were holding the blanket in such a way that it formed a kind of safety net. Do you get it now? All I had to do was let go of the limb and fall into the net.

"Come on, Hank. Jump! Jump! We'll catch you."

Great plan. Great idea. It had just one small flaw. When push came to shovel, I found that— oh boy, this is very embarrassing. How can I say this without creating the impression that—

Let's just blunder into it and see where it leads. Dogs are afraid of heights, right? I mean, we've already discussed that, but maybe we should underscore and underline and emphasize that this is no ordinary fear. It's a *terrible* fear! It's so severe that it even has a scientific name. It's called . . . Fallophobia.

I saw their faces looking up at me. They were waiting. Loper yelled, "Hank, for crying in the bucket, will you just let go?"

And Sally May muttered, "I knew it. It was too easy. That dog . . ."

Okay, shall we skip down to the bottom line? The bottom line is that Fallophobia is . . . uh . . . slightly irrational. I mean, with the thinking part of my mind I could see that this was a great plan and that it would work. If I would merely release my grip on the limb, I would fall into the blanket, and that would be the end of it.

But there is another side of a dog's mind, this one quite a bit darker and . . . well, more mysterious, shall we say, and that's where all the phobias stay. And that part of my mind saw this deal in a very different way, and it was sending out a stream of data and messages, such as:

"Are you crazy?"

"Do I look like a fool?"

"Forget that, Charlie!"

"Hey, this tree isn't going anywhere, and neither am I."

So, as you can see, we were on the road to getting ourselves into an . . . uh . . . awkward situation. I mean, I knew it was awkward. I knew what they wanted me to do, but . . .

Sigh. I just couldn't bring myself to let go of the limb. But don't forget: I felt terrible about it. No kidding.

Well, they dropped the blanket and began muttering and grumbling. Maybe they thought I couldn't hear them, but I did. Slim kicked a rock and said, "Well, if the dufus likes that tree so much, let's just leave him up there."

That brought a lip-quiver from Little Alfred. "No! He's my doggie and my fwiend, and I want to save him!"

There was a long silence. Then Loper turned to

Slim. "I guess one of us will have to climb the tree."

Slim nodded. "Yalp, and I'm dying to hear who that might be."

"Well, you're young, strong, athletic—"

"Uh-huh. Keep going."

"And idle time has always been a problem for you."

"Uh-huh. Keep going."

Loper smiled. "And I'm the boss."

"I figured it would come down to that." Slim hitched up his jeans and gave Loper a sour look. "When I hired onto this outfit, somebody said it would be a cowboy job. Here I am, climbing dad-gum trees to save a dog that ain't worth eight eggs."

He started up the tree. I think he could have climbed the tree without making all those grunting noises, and without mumbling all those threats. I mean, what was the big deal about climbing a tree to save a loyal friend in distress? But the way he grumbled and grunted, you'd have thought he was climbing up the Vampire State Building.

But don't forget that I felt terrible about this. I did. I mean, when I'd signed on with Alfred's pirate crew, I'd never dreamed . . . oh well.

Slim grunted his way up to the platform. There, he stopped to pull some splinters out of his arms. (Was it my fault that he'd gotten splinters? No, but guess who got blamed for it.) And he just happened to look up at the sky and noticed . . .

My goodness, it appeared that storm clouds were gathering—big dark thunderheads that rolled way up into the sky. Loper saw them too.

"Slim," he called out, "I know that hurrying up goes against your nature, but I don't think you want to be in that tree if lightning starts popping."

Slim nodded, then glared at . . . why was he glaring at me? Had I ordered a storm? Did he think I wanted to be . . .

"Pooch, if I get killed by lightning, I'm going to come back as a flea and set up a drilling rig right on your . . ."

At that very moment, his boot slipped and he came within an inch of falling out of the tree. I won't say that it served him right. I'll say only that it forced him to concentrate on his business and to stop muttering threats at me.

He grabbed the limb. Down on the ground, Loper yelled, "Shake the limb! If you can shake him loose, we'll catch him in the blanket." Thunder rumbled in the cloud. "And hurry, first chance you get."

Slim planted his feet and started shaking the limb.

Wham, wham, wham!

The limb shook and trembled. Out on the end,

I felt myself being thrashed and tossed around. My teeth rattled inside my mouth. My eyeballs were rolling around in their sprockets.

And, yipes! My paws were slipping! I was losing the grip of my grasp! I turned my eyes to the ground and saw—

There, three thousand feet below, was the blanket, only now it seemed as small as a postage stamp.

"Hank, you birdbrain, let go!"

Let go? Was he crazy?

Maybe, if he'd kept shaking the limb, things might have worked themselves out. Maybe he would have shaken me loose, or maybe I would have conquered my terrible Fallophobia. But just then . . .

# CHAPTER ELEVEN

# Just What We Needed: Buzzards

You won't believe this.

Who would have dreamed that two buzzards would land in the same tree that contained one dog and one cowboy? Not me. I mean, normal buzzards are shy about humans and go out of their way to keep away from them, right?

That's the way it's supposed to work, but guess who showed up. Wallace and Junior. They came flapping down out of the sky and crash-landed in the tree, right above me.

Slim froze and stared up at the big ugly birds. His mouth dropped open. All he could say was "Good honk! We're drawing buzzards."

Slim couldn't hear the buzzards talking (humans don't speak Buzzard), but I could.

101

Wallace yelled, "Here we go, son! A safe haven, one step ahead of the storm."

"Y-y-yeah, b-but P-p-pa, I think w-w-we've got c-c-company."

It was then that Wallace's buzzard eyes fell upon me. "Well, I never—Junior, what is that thing out there on that limb?"

Junior grinned. "W-w-well, I th-think it's our d-d-doggie f-f-friend, doggie friend."

"Doggie friend! Junior, there's two things wrong with that. In the first place, buzzards don't make friends with dogs, and in the second place, dogs don't climb trees. I'm sorry, son, but you need to get your glasses fixed."

"Y-y-yeah, b-b-but I d-d-don't wear gl-glasses."

"Well, maybe you should. That ain't a dog."

"I-i-i-is t-too a d-d-dog."

"It ain't a dog! Junior, don't argue with your . . ." Wallace squinted his eyes and gave me a closer inspection. "Well now, he does look kindly like a dog, don't he?"

"Y-y-yeah, 'cause h-h-he is."

"All right, maybe he's a dog, but he's no friend of ours. Junior, what do you reckon he's doing up here, dogs don't climb . . . son, tell that dog to scram out of here and leave us in peace!"

Junior gave me a smile and waved his wing.

"H-h-hi, d-d-doggie. Wh-what you d-d-doing up in this t-t-t-tree, tree?"

"I can't explain it, Junior. All I can tell you is that I'm here, and you can tell your old man that I've got no plans for leaving."

Junior shrugged and turned to the old man. "P-p-pa, he s-s-said—"

"I heard him, I heard him." Wallace whipped his head around and glared at me. "Pooch, I don't believe in sharing trees with with a dog. It ain't natural."

"Then leave."

"No sir, we ain't a-going to leave. There's a storm coming and we don't fly in bad weather, no we don't, so maybe we'll have to share this tree, is what we'll have to do."

"Fine with me."

Wallace tucked his head under his wing. "Junior, I'm fixing to take myself a nap. Tell that dog to lie still and shut up, 'cause if he wakes me up, I'm liable to be in a real cranky mood."

"O-o-okay, P-pa." Junior turned to me. "P-p-pa s-s-said . . ."

Just then, Slim climbed out on the limb and gave it another shake. "Hank, let go!"

I held on and rode it out, but all that shaking disturbed Wallace. His head came out from under his wing and he shot me a hot glare. "Dog, you was warned about making noise and carrying on. If this nonsense don't stop right now, I'm liable to get on the peck."

The old buzzard went back into his sleeping position. A moment later, Slim gave the limb another shake. Wallace's head shot up and his eyes were on fire.

"All right, that done it! Dog, you are fixing to—"

"P-p-pa, it w-w-wasn't the d-d-doggie. It w-w-was..." Junior aimed a wing at Slim. "...h-h-h-him."

Wallace's head swiveled around. "Well, who is he and what's he doing in my tree?"

"W-w-well, I th-think he's t-t-trying to h-h-help our d-d-doggie f-f-friend g-g-get out of the t-t-tree, tree, is h-h-how it l-l-looks to m-m-me."

"Help him." Wallace cut his eyes from side to side, then a big smile spread across his beak. "Why Junior, our doggie friend is in trouble, serious trouble! He might fall to the ground and—Junior, when was the last time we had a nice warm meal?"

"W-w-well, l-l-let me th-th-think . . ."

"It was two weeks ago, a dead rat on the side of the road, and son, this could be—rattle the tree, Junior, let's help that fine man, jump up and down! Supper's a-waiting! Go on, doggie, take a dive!"

Grinning like a lunatic, Wallace started jumping up and down on the limb. Slim hadn't under-

stood any of Wallace's conversation, and I don't
know what he thought was going on, but he inched
his way farther out on the limb and gave it a ferocious shake.

Once again, my teeth rattled. My ears flew in
all directions. Leaves and cottonwood cotton filled
the air. But through it all, I managed to hang on.

"Hank, let go of the dadgum . . . !"

CRACK!

Oops. I guess Slim went farther out on that limb than he should have. I could have told him. I mean, anyone with half a brain should have known . . .

Anyway, the limb broke. And fellers, you talk about things happening fast, and a situation going from bad to worse!

Maybe you think the limb broke in half and that Slim and I plunged to our deaths on the ground below. Or maybe you think Loper and Sally May and Alfred caught us in their safety net, and we all laughed and walked away.

Neither one.

Here's what happened. The limb broke, but it wasn't a clean break. Why? Because it was a green limb, and green limbs never break smooth in half, for the simple reason that—there's a simple explanation for it, but we don't have time to go into it.

And besides, I don't know the simple explanation.

The limb cracked, see, but held together by a hinge of green wood. That was the good news. The bad news was that the limb went from pointing straight out to pointing straight *down*, and all at once we found ourselves in a very odd situation.

I managed, through brute strength and determination, to cling to the limb, and we're talking about hugging that rascal with all four legs and paws. The limb swung back and forth, and I swung around, just barely hanging on. When I dared to open my eyes, I saw—

YIPES!

Guess who else was clinging to the limb with all his might, and whose face was now only six inches from the end of my nose.

Give up?

It was Slim, and boy, did he look . . . well, mad enough to commit destruction on someone, but he was so busy hanging on for dear life that he wasn't able to do what he was thinking.

It was a . . . uh . . . very awkward moment. I mean, I felt terrible about it, for I understood that in a small but tiny way, I had been . . . well, partly responsible for . . . I mean, he was hanging upside down on a half-broken limb, and if the limb happened to break the rest of the way . . .

The situation was not only awkward and embarrassing for poor Slim but also pretty dangerous. Your ordinary dogs would have done nothing to help. They would have just hung there, worrying about saving their own skins.

Me? I've always aimed for a higher standard, don't you know, and I've always been the kind of dog who cares deeply about the health and welfare of his human friends. What I did next was very risky, extremely dangerous and hazardous and . . . okay, courageous, let's go ahead and say it. I had to take bold action.

Risking life and limb (life and *limb*, get it?), I dared to shoot out my tongue and give poor Slim a lick on the nose, just to let him know that . . . hey, there was someone on the ranch who *really cared*.

My goodness, I think he . . . uh . . . missed the point. I mean, I was just trying to . . . you know what he did? All at once he clenched his teeth and his eyes bulged out so far that I could see twenty-three blood vessels in the white part.

And then he hissed, "Hank, if I get out of here alive . . . !"

Gee whiz, sometimes I get the feeling that it's impossible to please these people. I mean, you knock yourself out to . . .

All at once, the wind picked up again, a cool damp breeze coming from the southwest. The limb rocked back and forth, wider and wider, and on every swing, we could hear the squeak of the broken hinge.

Creak, creak, creak!

Then we were shaken by a big clap of thunder, so loud that it caused the wild turkeys to start gobbling down along the creek. (Was that some kind of clue? Don't forget about the Murphy Turkey Case.)

Pretty scary, huh? It got worse.

A big raindrop splatted me on the face. And then another. Good grief, it was starting to rain!

And from somewhere above me, I could hear the voice of an insane buzzard. "Jump, pooch! It ain't the fall that kills you, it's the sudden stop, ha ha! Junior, did you bring any salt and pepper?"

"P-p-pa, y-you ought to b-b-be ash-ash-ashamed of yourself."

"Yeah, but I ain't. Stand by for grub, son!"

The rain fell harder. My claws were getting wet. I could feel them slipping and losing their grip on the limb.

Down below, I could see Loper and Sally May and Alfred. They stared at me with wide, terror-filled eyes, and you know what? They were all upside down!

I was slipping . . . slipping . . . slipping . . .

I lost my grip.

I fell.

And I guess that's the end of the story.

Sorry.

# CHAPTER TWELVE

# Does It End Happily or in Tragedy?

**H**ey, I've already told you that the story's over. It ended in a tragic accident, when I plunged out of a huge cottonwood tree and blasted a six-foot crater in the ground below.

So how come you turned the page and went looking for another chapter?

Heh heh.

Okay, maybe this didn't turn out to be the Absolute End of my long and glorious career, and maybe I didn't get splattered all over the ranch. But I came real close.

Here's what happened, and this is the straight scoop. Loper, Sally May, and Little Alfred were standing at the base of the tree, remember? And they were staring up at me and Slim, and

110

they were too shocked and scared to move.

Oh, and don't forget that they were standing upside down. Or seemed to be.

Well, when Loper saw that I was slipping and losing my grip on the limb, he said, "Grab the blanket!"

The limb, the precious limb, slipped out of my claws and I plunged four thousand feet toward the hard ground below. As I heard the air rushing past my ears and waited for the terrible crunch that would end it all, my thoughts flew back over the years of my life and I saw the faces of all the many women and lady dogs who had loved and adored me . . .

Missy Coyote, Miss Scamper the Beagle, that cute Irish Setter in Twitchell, Trudy the Cocker Spaniel, and . . . sigh . . . yes, there she was, a glowing vision in the back of my mind—the lovely, incomparable Miss Beulah the Collie!

Ah, sweet Beulah! Her life would be a struggle, without me, but maybe she would find the courage to . . .

PLOP!

I blinked my eyes and looked up into three faces above me: Loper, Sally May, and Little Alfred. Holy smokes, you'll never believe . . .

Get this. Somehow they had turned themselves

right-side up, snatched the blanket up, pulled it tight, and moved it into the path of my fatal plunge! No kidding, and I had landed right in the middle of their safety net! Oh happy day! And now . . .

Gee whiz, wasn't anybody going to celebrate? I mean, they just dropped the blanket, forgot about the Head of Ranch Security, and now they were all staring up at . . . okay, Slim's situation was still pretty grim. I mean, there he was, hanging upside down and clutching a limb that was swinging back and forth in the wind. Wide, wild swings.

*And nobody had the slightest idea how to help him!*

Loper's eyes darted around. "Hon, what can we do?"

Sally May gave her head a shake. "I don't know. I don't think the blanket would break his fall, would it?"

Loper shook his head. "Slim, if we ran to the house and pulled a mattress off a bed, could you hang on until we got back?"

Slim shook his head, causing his hat to fall to the ground. "Don't think so. I'm losing my grip."

Loper chewed his lip and thought. "What if I drove the pickup around and parked it right here? If you landed on the top of the cab, it might break your fall."

"Or my neck. But I guess you could try. Just hurry!"

Loper made a dash for the pickup. Could Slim hang on? We waited in the deadly, brittle silence—only it wasn't really a silence, because now we could here the roar of a gigantic storm coming down the Wolf Creek valley.

Up in the tree, Slim said, "If that storm hits, I won't be able to . . ."

He didn't finish the sentence, but we all knew what he meant.

I darted my gaze around our sad little group. Little Alfred buried his face in Sally May's dress. Sally May's gaze fell to the ground, she just couldn't watch. And Drover—he had collapsed and covered his eyes with his paws, worthless to the end.

The roar of the storm came closer and closer, a terrible roaring sound.

Loper dived into the pickup and hit the starter. The motor turned over . . . and over . . . and over. We heard Loper yell, "Start, you piece of junk!"

But it didn't start. The motor had flooded. Or something. What do I know about motors? It didn't start, that's all I can tell you, and it wasn't my fault.

Loper leaped out of the pickup and came running back to the tree. "It won't start, Slim! Hang on, maybe we'll think of something!"

Well, someone had to take charge, make some decisions, and provide some leadership to save our friend. This was a job for the Head of Ranch Security.

I took a gulp of air and stepped forward, and there, in front of everyone, I took the kind of bold action we so desperately needed.

I barked.

Yes sir, I barked! And this was no ordinary barking. These were the kind of deep thunderous barks we save for the very seriousest and emergenciest—for the very most serious of emergency situations. These were the kind of barks that have such a powerful recoil, they knock a dog back three steps on every shot.

Oh, you should have seen me! I barked the base of the tree, I barked the top of the tree, and I even barked encouragement to poor Slim. And then, with the roar of the storm coming straight at us, I even turned and dared to bark at the storm itself!

A lot of dogs wouldn't have had the nerve to do that—stand their ground, face the roar of the terrible storm, and fire barks right into the middle of it. But I did. And you know what?

It worked.

*I saved Slim!*

You don't believe me? You think I'm just making it up? Ha! Listen to this.

Okay, the storm was bearing down on us, right? Roaring down the valley, and we're talking about a dark curtain of rain, exactly the kind of rain that could wash a grown man right out of a tree.

Did I run and hide? Did I quiver and moan? No sir. I stiffened my back and fired off round after round of Anti-storm Barkings. Those barks were so powerful, they penetrated the dark rolling clouds and actually . . .

This is the good part, so pay close attention.

Those barks went up into the clouds and gave them such a shake, it shook loose a bolt of lighting. No kidding. Honest. And that bolt of lightning came crashing down from the sky, struck the tree with a huge BOOM, and cut it in two!

Yes sir, it was the old Lightning Trick, and I'd saved it for exactly this kind of emergency. It cut the tree smooth in half, and the half that Slim was in just . . . *sank to the ground*!

It didn't fall. It didn't crash to the ground. It just sank and landed as softly as . . . something. A feather drifting down to earth, I suppose.

Old Slim blinked and looked around with big round eyes. He struggled to his feet, picked up his hat, and slapped it on his head. And then, would you believe that he turned to me and said, "Hank, you just saved my life. Why, if you hadn't called down that bolt of lightning, I'd have been buzzard bait. I'll personally see that you get a hero's reward for this."

Can you believe that? Well, don't bother trying, because it never happened. It should have, and in a perfect world, it would have. But, to be honest, Slim didn't have time to say much of anything, because just then, the storm hit—wind, sheets of rain, thunder, lightning, the whole nine yards.

Slim and the others made a dash for the house, and Drover and I took cover in the calf shed. There, as we watched the water pouring off the tin roof, I told Drover the whole story. He'd missed it all, you know, because he'd been too much of a weenie to watch.

He was very impressed. "You mean . . . gosh, you did all that? All by yourself?"

"That's correct. I hated to take such drastic measures, but knocking that lightning out of the clouds was our last chance to save Slim. It had to be done."

"Wow! Maybe you can teach me how to bark like that."

I gave the little mutt a fatherly smile. "Maybe so, Drover, maybe so."

I didn't have the heart to tell him that his yipping and squeaking would never work on one of your major spring thunderstorms.

And that's about all the story. The next day, the cowboys cranked up their chain saws and cut up the tree into firewood. Captain Alfred lost his ship and also his command, and got a stern lecture from his momma about playing Pirate Ship in trees.

Did I get any medals of honor, decorations, or even extra dog food for saving Slim's life? No, but that wasn't exactly a surprise. When you're Head of Ranch Security, you do your job and go on with life, knowing that good work is its own reward.

To tell you the truth, I'm not sure that Slim ever made the connection between my Heroic Barking Episode and lightning striking the tree. Can you believe that?

There are *so many things* that humans don't understand.

Oh well. I had saved Slim's life, that's what really mattered, even if he never knew it or thanked me for it.

The storm passed and the ranch returned to its normal sounds and rhythms. By six o'clock that evening, Drover and I were back to work on another case. See, we'd noticed that the wild turkeys were behaving in a very suspicious manner—one big tom turkey in particular. We noticed that he was *lurking* around the gas tanks, see, and I sent Drover out on a very important mission to—

Have we discussed this case before? I don't think so, but there's something familiar . . . hmmm. Anyway, Drover returned with the shocking news: the turkeys were plotting a rebellion, led by a secret agent named Murphy! He had penetrated our security . . .

But that's another adventure, and we'll take it up another time.

Case closed.

The following activities are samples from *The Hank Times*, the official newspaper of Hank's Security Force. Do not write on these pages unless this is your book. Even then, why not just find a scrap of paper?

# Eye-Crosserosis

I've done it again. I was staring at the end of my nose and had my eyes crossed for a long time. And you know what? They got hung up—my eyes, I mean. I couldn't get them uncrossed. It's a serious condition called Eye-Crosserosis. (You can read about the big problems Eye-Crosserosis caused me in my second book.) This condition throws everything out of focus, as you can see. Can you help me turn the double letters and word groupings below into words?

Insert the double letters into the word groupings to form words you can find in my books.

|  |  |  |  |  |  |
|---|---|---|---|---|---|
| OO | NN | PP | CC | TT | LL |
| SS | ZZ | RR | FF | EE | OO |

**1.** HAY_____

**2.** TTHPICK_____

**3.** KIY_____

**4.** AUAL_____

**5.** PULE_____

**6.** WD___WOOD_____

**7.** COECT_____

**8.** SKIET_____

**9.** TTH_____

**10.** DEERT_____

**11.** AIDENT_____

**12.** BLUING_____

# Rhyme Time

If Hank the Cowdog got his archenemy Pete the Barncat to leave the ranch, what would Pete do? Would he have to look for a job? What jobs could Pete do?

*Example:* Pete could open a sandwich shop and name it this: PETE'S EATS

1. Pete could be the commander of a bunch of big boats.
2. Pete could be something found on your bed.
3. Pete becomes an echo and does this when you say something.
4. Pete becomes freezing rain.
5. Pete could become the computer key that gets rid of mistakes.
6. Pete becomes a farmer and plants this type of grain.
7. Pete invents some special kinds of Halloween candy.
8. Pete invents some new track running shoes.
9. Pete invents a secret handshake.
10. Pete could become the sun and make us feel this.

# "Photogenic" Memory Quiz

**W**e all know that Hank has a "photogenic" memory—being aware of your surroundings is an important quality for a Head of Ranch Security. Now you can test your powers of observation.

How good is your memory? Look at the illustration on page 39 and try to remember as many things about it as possible. Then turn back to this page and see how many questions you can answer.

**1.** Which paw did Drover have over his face?

**2.** Did the door have a knob or a handle?

**3.** Was Hank sitting on the ground, on the first step, or on the second step?

**4.** Was Alfred wearing a boot?

**5.** Was Alfred's eyepatch over his left eye or his right eye?

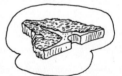

**6.** Which leg did Alfred have the peg leg attached to—his left or his right?

# Have you read all of Hank's adventures?

□ Yes, I want to join Hank's Security Force. Enclosed is $12.95 ($8.95 + $4.00 for shipping and handling) for my **two-year member-ship**. [Make check payable to Maverick Books.]

**Which book would you like to receive in your Welcome Package? Choose any book in the series.**

(#          )          (#          )

FIRST CHOICE          SECOND CHOICE

**BOY or GIRL**

YOUR NAME          (CIRCLE ONE)

MAILING ADDRESS

CITY          STATE     ZIP

TELEPHONE          BIRTH DATE

E-MAIL

Are you a □ Teacher or □ Librarian?

**Send check or money order for $12.95 to:**

Hank's Security Force
Maverick Books
P.O. Box 549
Perryton, Texas 79070

**DO NOT SEND CASH. NO CREDIT CARDS ACCEPTED.**
*Allow 4–6 weeks for delivery.*

*The Hank the Cowdog Security Force, the Welcome Package, and* The Hank Times *are the sole responsibility of Maverick Books. They are not organized, sponsored, or endorsed by Penguin Putnam Inc., Puffin Books, Viking Children's Books, or their subsidiaries or affiliates.*